Of Things Not Seen

Of Things Not Seen

DON AKER

Stoddart

Published in 1995 by
Stoddart Publishing Co. Limited
34 Lesmill Road
Toronto, Canada
M3B 2T6
Tel. (416) 445-3333
Fax (416) 445-5967

Stoddart Books are available for bulk purchase for sales
promotions, premiums, fundraising, and seminars. For details,
contact the **Special Sales Department** at the above address.

Canadian Cataloguing in Publication Data

Aker, Don, 1955–
Of things not seen

"A Gemini Book"
ISBN: 0-7736-7435-7

I. Title.

PS8551.K5404 1995   jC813'.54   C95-930633-1
PZ7.A540f 1995

Cover Design: Bill Douglas/The Bang
Cover Illustration: Albert Slark
Computer Graphics: Tannice Goddard/S.O. Networking
Printed and Bound in Canada

Stoddart Publishing gratefully acknowledges
the support of the Canada Council,
the Ontario Ministry of Culture, Tourism, and Recreation, Ontario Arts Council, and
Ontario Publishing Centre
in the development of writing and publishing in Canada.

For Deborah, Lauren, and Caitlin,
who believe the impossible
is just something that no one's done yet

Acknowledgements

I want to thank Leona Trainer for seeing promise in my early pages, and Lynne Missen and Kathryn Cole for their patience and expertise in guiding me through this first novel. Finally, loving thanks to my parents who gave me what all children should have.

1

". . . and suddenly the whole world was sound: glass shattering, metal grinding, twisting, bone cracking, splintering. The front bumper shrieked as it crumpled and was driven back through the grill, radiator, fan, motor. Both front tires burst simultaneously, and the bug-spattered windshield crashed inward like a single, solid wave. The speedometer needle, which a split second earlier had pointed at 120 km/h, now aimed itself at David's belly as the dash rose up and wrapped itself around the steering column in a sudden plastic embrace.

"Yet David was aware of none of this. His mind had not yet registered the impact of vehicle against bridge guardrail. He was unaware that his father's Buick was now in midair, plummeting towards the icy waters below. He was unaware that his heart would beat only twice more before it exploded in a chest crushed between front seat and steering wheel. All he knew was that his right hand no longer held the beer bottle he'd drunk from only moments before. And then he knew nothing."

Mr. Lewis looked up from the duotang he'd been reading, closed it, and said, "The end." He glanced at Ben Corbett who sat sideways in his seat at the back, facing the window. "Well done, Ben," the teacher said quietly.

There was a heartbeat of silence and then suddenly the classroom erupted as the grade elevens applauded and whistled and stomped their feet in approval. Eddie Saunders and Carl Zwicker reached over and slapped Ben on the back. Even Shay Phillips turned around and flashed him a thumbs-up.

Ben looked around the classroom, his face scarlet, and sought out Ann. Her eyes glistening, Ann smiled back at him and suddenly Ben could breathe again. He felt like he'd been underwater for the last fifteen minutes, drifting beneath a sea of his own words. Spoken aloud, they'd seemed fragile, disconnected from the world he'd tried to create between the blue lines on his loose-leaf. Listening to them, he had felt silly and exposed. He had agonized over how the class would respond to his story and regretted giving Mr. Lewis permission to read it.

Looking at Ann, though, Ben felt relief wash over him. Ann he could trust, even more than himself. She had told him the story was a good one — "Your best yet," she'd said, and she had been right.

Smiling, Mr. Lewis held up his hands and after a moment the whistling and applause died away. "Ben," he said, "'One for the Road' is a terrific piece of writing. If it's okay with you, I'd like to keep this copy so I can share it with my other classes."

His face burning, Ben nodded. As much as he'd wanted to say no, it seemed pointless to refuse. Mr. Lewis was a good teacher and Ben appreciated the genuine interest he showed in his students' work. Ben would miss him when this school year ended and he and his classmates moved on to another English teacher. But he wished this class would end now.

Then miraculously the final bell of the day rang, signalling the beginning of the Victoria Day weekend, the last long weekend of the school year. He bent down to retrieve his books from beneath his desk, then stood and moved towards the door with everyone else. Being a town student Ben could afford to take his time, unlike the bus students who raced for their lockers before launching themselves missile-like towards the buses that rumbled in the schoolyard.

Eddie Saunders was one of those bus students and he'd made it to the bottleneck at the door before Ben had even gotten out of his seat.

Looking back, Eddie called, "Jeez, Corbett, that was some story."

Ben flushed again and smiled awkwardly as Eddie disappeared into the crowd.

"He's right. That was some story."

Ben turned around and looked up at Shay Phillips, whose blond head was nearly four inches above his own. "Thanks." Standing there in second-hand jeans and a shirt his mother had bought at Frenchy's for three dollars, Ben didn't know what else to say. He always felt tongue-tied around Shay. The only son of two lawyers, Shay quite literally had everything: money, looks, intelligence, athletic ability, confidence. Everything. Ben had often wondered what it would be like to be Shay Phillips. Now he wondered what it would be like to say more than one syllable. Words that flowed so easily onto his paper always seemed to vanish when he was around people like Shay. Ben looked at his watch, suddenly absorbed in the snail-like sweep of the second hand beneath the scratched crystal, and he prayed the knot of people at the door would unravel and set him free.

As Ben came abreast of Mr. Lewis's desk, the teacher looked up from the papers he was sorting and putting into his knapsack. That was another thing Ben liked about Mr. Lewis — while most of the other teachers at Brookdale High carried leather briefcases, Mark Lewis came to school every day with an army surplus backpack slung over his shoulder. "Ben," Mr. Lewis said, "could I see you for a moment?"

Relieved, Ben held back and allowed Shay to pass him. "Sure," he said. He glanced over the students in front of him and saw Ann waiting just outside the door. He caught her eye and signalled for her to go on without him, putting his hand to his ear to show he'd call her later. Then he waited as the teacher finished packing up and tidying his desk. They were alone when Mr. Lewis finally spoke, and Ben got the feeling he had planned it that way.

"I want to thank you again for letting me read your story today, Ben. I know how hard it was for you to share it."

"How could you tell?"

The teacher smiled. "I recognize agony when I see it. Every time I turned a page, you winced."

Ben could feel his ears turning red and he grinned sheepishly. "It wasn't your reading —" he began, but Mr. Lewis interrupted him.

"I know. It's being so vulnerable. Like everyone is looking inside you, seeing things you're not really sure you want them to see."

Impressed, Ben nodded. "That's exactly how it felt."

"Have you felt that way all year when I've asked you to share your writing in your conference groups?"

"No. Not really." Ben paused for a moment, considering the difference. "In those situations, I chose the pieces that I wanted to share. And I got to choose the people I wanted to share them with." He thought of Ann, who was always in his group, and of Shay, who never was.

Mr. Lewis leaned forward in his chair. "The reason I'm asking," he said, "is that I'm wondering how you'd feel about sharing your writing with people you've never met before."

Ben blinked. "What do you mean?"

"You're a remarkable writer, Ben. Better than any other student I've encountered in my three years' teaching. Certainly better than I am. You have no idea how often I've read some of your pieces and wished I'd written them."

Ben thought about the glowing comments Mr. Lewis had written on his poems, stories, essays, and journal entries this year, comments Ben had re-read many times as he'd lain on his bed trying not to hear what was happening in the kitchen or the living room or the bedroom across the hall. Sometimes the teacher's written comments helped Ben shut out the sounds. Sometimes they didn't.

"I mean that, Ben," Mr. Lewis continued. "You're a gifted writer. And I'm not just talking about your knowledge of grammar and syntax. You have a writer's soul. You study people and situations and you notice details that most of us overlook. Then you weave these details into a reality of your own making, which ultimately is the reality we all experience, yet seldom see. I've learned far more from you this year than you have from me."

Ben's whole face was hot and he was sure his ears looked like dual stop lights. He was suddenly grateful Mr. Lewis had waited until everyone else had left. "Thank you," he mumbled.

The teacher waved away his words. "That's not just praise," he said. "It's the truth."

Embarrassed, Ben tried to change the subject. "You said something about sharing my writing with people I've never met."

The teacher reached into his desk and pulled out an envelope. He handed it to Ben. It was addressed to Mr. Lewis and Ben looked at him questioningly.

"Go on. Open it," said the teacher.

Inside was a letter typed on exquisite paper. At the top printed in gold script were the words "CANADIAN WRITERS' COUNCIL," followed by an Ottawa address and telephone number.

"Read it out loud," said Mr. Lewis, beaming broadly.

"Dear Mr. Lewis," Ben began. "As Chairman of the Canadian Writers' Council, I am pleased to inform you that your student, Mr. Benjamin Corbett, has been selected to participate in this year's Summer Institute for Young Writers to be held July 5-19." Ben stopped, his mouth open as he looked at the teacher.

Mr. Lewis's eyes twinkled and his smile, if possible, seemed even broader. "Keep reading."

Ben searched for the place he'd stopped, then began again. "Mr. Corbett was one of twenty students selected from over seven hundred applicants across the country. Along with the other members of the selection panel, I was impressed not only by the range of Mr. Corbett's ability, as demonstrated in the various forms of writing you submitted, but also by the depth of expression found throughout his work. In particular, we found his prose poem 'Walking Backwards' to be one of the most compelling pieces submitted by an applicant in the fourteen-year history of the competition. We are looking forward to meeting him and working with him this summer. You will find details about the Institute and our requirements for its participants in the information packet enclosed. Should you or Mr. Corbett have any further questions, please do not hesitate to phone us toll-free at the number above. Our congratulations to both of you. Sincerely, William Bradshaw."

The vortex of voices and locker noise in the hallway outside Mr. Lewis's room had subsided, and now through the classroom window came the hiss of air brakes being released as buses revved and rumbled out of the parking lot. But Ben was conscious of none of this. Like his character David in "One for the Road," Ben was, for the moment, aware of only one thing — the letter he held in his hands. He re-read it silently as if not believing that the name repeated so often in those few lines was his own.

Finally he looked up. "How —" It was all he could think of to say.

Mr. Lewis leaned back in his chair and put his hands palm-down on the big oak desk in front of him. "First, I owe you an apology. Five months ago, I submitted copies of several of your pieces to the Summer Institute competition."

Ben suddenly realized his mouth was open. He closed it. Then he opened it again. "But you've always told us —"

"I've always told my students that I'd never share their writing with someone else without first asking their permission. I know. And until now I haven't."

Ben knew this was true. There was no official writing text in Mr. Lewis's course. His "textbook" consisted of his students' writing, which he photocopied and distributed among his classes. Together, he and his students would identify what each writer had done well, then make suggestions each writer might consider when revising a piece. He never allowed discussions of someone's writing to be anything but positive and helpful. And he never distributed copies of a student's writing without first receiving permission. Until now.

"I'm sorry, Ben. Mr. Langley, our faculty chairman, received information about the competition in the fall and had given it to the grade twelve English teacher who was supposed to read it and then pass it along to the other members of the English department. Somehow the information got misplaced and didn't surface again until just before the Christmas break. The day I finally saw it was the application deadline date. The moment I read about the competition I knew you were the student whose work I wanted to enter, but you weren't in school that day. I tried to reach you on the phone but there was no answer, so I took the liberty of entering your work anyway. I planned to explain what I'd done when I saw you next, but you didn't return to school until after the holidays and by then it had slipped my mind. As a matter of fact, I didn't think about it again until I received that letter today." He pointed at the paper Ben still gripped in his hands. "I hope you'll forgive me."

The euphoria that had flooded Ben suddenly evaporated. He didn't want to be reminded of his absence from school in December. Or of any of the other absences that had happened at almost regular intervals over the years. Without realizing it he was frowning.

"Ben?" Mr. Lewis looked concerned. "You *will* forgive me, won't you? My intentions were good. I think the Summer Institute is a wonderful opportunity for you. Not only will it give you a chance to learn more about writing from some of the country's finest authors, but you'll also meet several publishers interested in discovering talented young writers like yourself. I think this is a chance of a lifetime."

Ben looked up and smiled wanly. "Hey, Mr. Lewis. You don't have to sell me. I want to thank you for entering me in the competition. I'm thrilled. Really." But his voice was flat, toneless.

Now it was the teacher's turn to frown. "You don't *sound* very thrilled," he said. "Are you worried about having to share your writing with strangers? Because you shouldn't be. I guarantee you that the other participants will be just as impressed by your work as I am."

"That's not it." Ben looked down at the letter, avoiding Mr. Lewis's eyes. "I won't be going."

Mr. Lewis leaned forward. "What do you mean you won't be going? Is it your parents? Won't they —"

"No." Ben looked at the gilded script at the top of the paper, the dramatic signature at the bottom, his own name typed so many times in between. He felt the smooth thickness of the expensive paper between his fingers, the knife-edge crease a secretary had made before putting it into the envelope he'd opened only a few minutes earlier. He would remember every detail of this moment for a long, long time. Every detail except one. He would try to forget the lie he was about to tell now. *Careful.* "I just don't want to."

Mr. Lewis raised his eyebrows. "You can't mean that, Ben. Why don't you want to go?"

Ben looked at Mr. Lewis's forehead. He could not meet the teacher's gaze. "Writing's fun, but I have a chance at a part-time job at Save-Easy over the summer. I don't want to give up two weeks' work for something that's just for fun."

Mr. Lewis shook his head in disbelief. Leaning back, he put his elbows on the arms of his chair and placed his hands together, fingertips lightly touching in a gesture that reminded Ben of the childhood finger game of the church and the steeple. "Ben," he said, his voice low, "I had no right to enter you in the competition without your permission, and your decision to attend the Institute or not is certainly yours to make. I'll respect it. I hope you'll reconsider, though. Opportunities like this don't come along often."

Ben handed the letter and the envelope back to Mr. Lewis, then picked up the books he'd set on the teacher's desk. "I really appreciate your interest, Mr. Lewis," he said quietly. "It was nice being one of the twenty who were chosen. I'm sorry you went to all that trouble for nothing." He moved towards the doorway.

"Ben?"

Ben was in the hallway when he turned. "Yes, Mr. Lewis?"

"At least think about it over the weekend."

"There's nothing to think about. Really. Thanks, anyway."

Mr. Lewis listened to Ben's footsteps echo down the empty hallway. Slow and shuffling at first, their pace increased until the teacher knew Ben was running by the time he reached the exit door.

2

Ben was still running long after he'd left the schoolyard behind. His breath came in ragged gasps and his ears ached with the steady THUDthud of his heartbeat, yet still he ran, his feet pounding the concrete sidewalk. His anger kept him going, anger that grew from resentment and frustration into a bright red bloom, blocking out everything but the concrete and his worn sneakers and the sounds both made when they came together.

He hadn't headed home. That was the last place he'd wanted to go. Without thinking he'd run in the opposite direction, down by Memorial Park, past the bridge that spanned the lazy Annapolis River, up through the oak-lined avenues of the new residential section of Brookdale called Empire Heights. Except for some kids on new bikes, Ben met few people on the sidewalks as he ran. Residents of Empire Heights who were Ben's age or older rarely used the sidewalks, most of them choosing to drive rather than walk. As if to prove the point, a Volvo, a BMW, and a silver Lexus swept by in rapid succession, the first two driven by well-dressed women about Ben's mother's age. Behind the wheel of the Lexus sat a grade twelve student Ben recognized from school. Ben pushed himself harder, ran even faster until, finally, he could run no more.

He stumbled to a stop and bent over, wheezing, his chest in a fiery vise. He dropped his books on the sidewalk and put his hands on his knees, his wet palms sticky against his jeans. Sweat ran in little rivers from his scalp down his neck and face, some of it burning his eyes before dropping to the sidewalk. His shirt was dark with perspiration under his arms and down his back, and he could already smell the sour sweetness of it as he stood in the hot May sunshine. His legs felt swollen and spongy like wet wood ready to collapse under its own weight. Trembling with exhaustion, he slumped down on the grass at the edge of a manicured lawn, soft and lush beneath tall oak trees.

I am pleased to inform you . . .

I was impressed not only by the range of Mr. Corbett's ability . . .

We found his prose poem "Walking Backwards" to be one of the most compelling . . .

We are looking forward to meeting him and . . .

The words flashed again and again across Ben's mind like lighthouse beacons stabbing darkness. He could still see the paper on which those words were printed, could still feel the excitement that had welled up inside him as they'd formed in his mouth, could still hear his own voice as he'd spoken them aloud. Those words he'd first thought had been written about someone else. Some other Ben Corbett who'd been chosen from over seven hundred applicants. Some other Ben Corbett who wrote prose poems and short stories and essays on things that mattered. Some other Ben Corbett who actually could have attended the Summer Institute in Ottawa.

For a moment he had been that other Ben Corbett. For just a moment.

Then had come the knowing, crashing down on him like a cold wave made of other words — Mr. Lewis's words.

I tried to reach you on the phone . . .

There was no answer . . .

You didn't return to school . . .

And he was again the Ben Corbett who sometimes missed school for days at a time. The Ben Corbett who lived in the tiny bungalow on North Street across from Freemont's Lumber Yard. The Ben Corbett whose mother worked part-time as a cashier at the Brookdale Save-Easy. The Ben Corbett whose stepfather liked plenty of beer in the fridge, supper on the table at 5:30, and the sound his fists made when anything interfered with whatever else he wanted.

Ann was the only person who knew this Ben Corbett. Oh, sure, everyone at school *thought* they knew him, the quiet, dark-haired sixteen-year-old whose family had moved to Brookdale a year and a half ago. Ben had hated starting all over again, the fifth time in as many years. Jim Rankin, his stepfather, had moved them here from Rockport, Guysborough County, to find work. At least, that's what his mother had told Lou Eisner, their landlord, the morning they'd left.

They had lived in Rockport less than a year.

Ben's first day at Brookdale High had become a series of mental photographs, some blurred like the sea of faces he'd passed in the hallways on his way to register at the office, some crystalline like the moment outside his homeroom just before Mr. Branigan introduced him to his class. His heart had hammered against his chest until he was sure it could be seen beating beneath his worn denim shirt, and he'd tugged continually at his sleeves to make sure they covered his wrists. He'd looked at no one when he entered the room and he'd been glad the only available seat was in the far corner at the back. It was only as he sat down that he allowed himself to glance up at the people nearby. Many of them had turned around and were smiling at him, nodding their heads. One, a tall, blond, athletic-looking student sitting one row over and two seats up, faced forward, not once looking back.

Moving to a new school was hard enough anytime, but arriving in the second month of the school year after friendships and cliques had already been established was something Ben had dreaded. Not that he'd left friends behind in Rockport. It was easier being a loner. It meant you didn't have to explain as much, or as often. But being new in October made it harder not to be noticed. He was the topic of a lot of conversations at Brookdale High, like the one he'd overheard in the library the week after he'd arrived.

He'd gone to the library during noon hour to escape being The New Guy for a while, and he'd hidden himself away in a study carrel with a book of short stories by Raymond Carver, Ben's favourite author. The page Carver wrote on was the mind of his reader — there was as much story in what Carver *didn't* include between his first and last sentences as there was in the words he actually wrote. Ben liked the idea of not having to say it all.

He was in the middle of "A Small, Good Thing" when Alison Myers and a girl named Sandy or Cindy, two people in his history class, came in and sat at a table near the window just across from his carrel. It had been pouring outside, sheets of water slapping the glass while thunder rolled in the distance, but Ben could hear them easily as they sat looking out at the October rain, speaking in low tones.

"I'm dying for a cigarette," Alison whispered, glancing over at Mrs. Croft. When she was sure the librarian wasn't looking, she took a pack of

Juicy Fruit out of her jeans pocket and popped a stick into her mouth. She gave one to her friend.

"Thanks," Sandy or Cindy said as she slipped the gum out of its wrapper and into her mouth, making sure that Mrs. Croft's eyes were still directed elsewhere. "I could stand a smoke now, too, but you'd have to be crazy to go out in that today." She nodded at the wind and rain that made their view of the soccer field look like the inside of a washing machine.

One of the first things the vice-principal had told Ben when he'd registered at Brookdale was that the school was smoke-free. That, however, hadn't seemed to stop the large group of teenagers often huddled together on the sidewalk just off the school grounds. That day, though, only a handful of the most hard-core smokers had braved the outdoors for the two or three drags the rain allowed them before soaking their cigarettes.

"Does that new guy smoke?" asked Alison.

Her friend shook her head. "I don't think so. I asked him if I could borrow a cigarette from him the other day but he said he didn't have any. And I've never seen him out on the walk."

Alison unzipped a cloth case and rummaged around inside, finally taking out a brush. As she ran it through her long straight hair, the librarian shot her a disapproving look, making it clear she believed personal grooming better suited to bathrooms than book repositories. Alison just smiled at her, her jaws immobile.

When Mrs. Croft had turned away, the two girls

began chewing again. "What do you think of him?" Alison whispered.

"Who?"

Alison rolled her eyes. "Who were we just talking about, dummy? The new guy."

"Oh. Him." She shrugged her shoulders. "Seems nice enough. Doesn't say much, though, does he?"

"Not unless you ask him a direct question," Alison agreed. "Even then he doesn't answer right away." She chewed her gum thoughtfully. "It's like he takes his time choosing every word, like he wants to make sure whatever comes out of his mouth is exactly what he wants to say."

"I know what you mean. Funny."

Ben felt his face flush and he turned back to "A Small, Good Thing," re-reading sentences that suddenly made no sense. He wanted to leave but he didn't want the girls to see him, didn't want them to know he'd overheard.

There was a pause. Then, "He's kind of cute."

"Yeah, he is. I wish he wouldn't wear his hair down over his forehead like that, though. It's always in his eyes. He reminds me of my uncle's sheepdog."

Alison giggled.

"Girls." The librarian's voice was sharp, almost nasal, as it echoed across the room. "Need I remind you that a library is for working?"

"No, Mrs. Croft," replied Sandy or Cindy, but under her breath she muttered, "Dinkweed."

Alison snorted and suddenly the two were laughing aloud — at Mrs. Croft, at the rain, at the cigarettes in their handbags that weren't getting smoked. Before the librarian could scold them again, the girls pushed their chairs back and gathered up their things and left.

Alone in his carrel, Ben had closed his book and put his head in his hands, his fingers touching the scar just above his right eye.

* * * *

Without knowing it, Ben was rubbing that scar now, the tips of his fingers tracing the ragged semicircle between his eyebrow and his right temple. He'd told the doctor who stitched him up in Outpatients that he'd fallen off a bike. He wouldn't look at his mother who stood beside the high table-like bed, her face drawn and grey.

"You could have lost your eye," the doctor had said. "You were lucky."

Yeah, real lucky, he thought as he sat on that perfect Empire Heights lawn beneath perfect oak trees. Lucky to have a father who ran out on us before I was six. Lucky to live hand-to-mouth while Mom tried to support us. Lucky to have a man like Jim Rankin marry her seven years ago and put a roof over our heads. Real lucky. Life is one golden opportunity after another.

He remembered the Summer Institute and Mr. Lewis saying, "Opportunities like this don't come along often." No, they don't, he thought and angrily tore at the grass beneath his fingers. Especially for people like Ben Corbett.

"Hey! What are you doing there?"

Ben twisted around to see a man standing on the paved driveway behind him. He wore a freshly pressed business suit and carried a leather brief-case. He was frowning.

Ben stood up, the backs of his legs muttering about the soreness he knew would set in later. "Nothing," he said. "Just resting."

"And pulling out my grass while you're at it!" the man snarled.

Ben looked down at his hands to see thick tufts of green gripped between his fingers. Mortified, he opened his palms and let the grass fall to his feet. "I . . . I'm sorry. I didn't mean to. I . . . " Ben paused, groping for something more to say. "I was thinking about something else."

"That's prime bluegrass you were ripping out. Sod trucked down from Ontario. Cost over fifteen bucks a square metre. Maybe you could think about *that* the next time you feel like tearing up someone's lawn."

"I'm sorry," Ben repeated. He bent down and picked up his books, wondering how long he'd been sitting there. He didn't want to be late. There were chores waiting for him, chores that had to be done before Rankin got home.

"You've got some gall destroying private property!"

Ben looked up. The man was striding across the lawn towards him. Instinctively, Ben pulled his shoulders in, bracing himself. "It was only a little grass —" he began, but by now the man towered over him, his face red, his eyes dark and flashing, and there was nothing more Ben could say.

"Where do you live?" His voice was sharp, whip-like.

"H-here," Ben stammered.

The man's eyes flickered over Ben's clothing. "The Heights?" he sneered. It was more a statement of disbelief than a question.

Ben felt blood rise to his cheeks. "Uh, no. Here in Brookdale."

Somewhere in front of Ben, blocked from view by the man, a door opened and closed.

"*Where* in Brookdale? I want to call your parents!"

Ben's heart somersaulted twice and his ears roared with the hot rush of gut-fall. "No! Please!" Ben heard himself pleading and hated himself for it. "I'll pay for it!"

"It's not the money," the man growled. "You teenagers need to be taught respect. This isn't a park, you know. I pay a hell of a lot in taxes for what you see here." He waved his hand indicating the property behind him, and for the first time Ben was aware of the house he'd chosen to sit in front of. A two-storey colonial in brick and blue clapboards, it had a three-car garage attached by a breezeway through which Ben could see a pool sparkling in the backyard. Vines grew everywhere, even climbing a trellis attached to a massive chimney that contained at least two fireplaces. It was a magnificent house. The bungalow Ben's family rented could probably fit inside its living room.

Suddenly Ben realized there was someone standing on the front step directly behind the man, watching them. He wanted desperately to be away from there, to turn and run, but he willed his feet to stay where they were. "I'm really sorry, sir. You're right. You've got a nice place here." He was talking fast, all the while trying to hear himself above the pounding of his heart. "I was wrong to do that to your grass. I promise it won't happen again."

The man looked him up and down, then shook his head. Ben could see disgust in his eyes, could hear it in his voice. "You be sure it doesn't." He almost spat the words. "Now get out of here."

Ben nodded and turned to leave. In the act of turning, though, he froze.

"I said get out of here!"

Ben began to run, his books slapping his side as his arms pumped the air. Trees and houses sped by as he pounded along the sidewalk, but he saw nothing, heard nothing, his mind a whirl of emotions. He tried not to think about what would happen if he was late getting his chores done. He tried not to think about the trouble he'd almost got into back there in Empire Heights. But most of all, he tried not to think about the person he'd seen in that final moment when he'd turned to leave. Tall, blond, immaculate in white tennis shorts and polo shirt. It was Shay Phillips.

3

"Rachel?"

"Up here."

Mark Lewis stepped around the Coleman cooler in the middle of the kitchen floor and followed his wife's voice up the stairs. He found her in their bedroom, packing clothes into a gym bag that doubled as a suitcase when they went camping.

"I've almost finished," she said as he leaned over and kissed her. "I washed your blue sweater. Do you want to take it?"

"Thanks. I'd better," he said. "The forecast doesn't look good. Probably be cold at night." They'd gone camping at Kejimkujik National Park every Victoria Day weekend since they'd met four years ago. They both loved the outdoors, and Keji had thirty-eight thousand hectares of woodland, lakes, rivers, and hiking trails. They had spent their honeymoon there.

"Did you have any trouble getting away from the bank early?" he asked, taking off his school clothes and pulling on faded jeans and a T-shirt.

"I worked through lunch and Brenda said she'd cover for me if anything unexpected came up." She added the sweater, which she'd bought Mark at L. L. Bean the summer they camped in Maine, to the bulging gym bag and zipped it closed. "All set," she said. She turned to see her husband still standing by the bed. He was staring at an envelope he held in his hand. "What's that?"

He looked up. "A letter I got at school today." He'd shoved it into his pocket after his meeting with Ben. He hadn't known what else to do with it.

"Who's it from?"

He passed it to her. "Here, read it."

She opened it and, as her eyes moved down the page, they widened in surprise. "This is *terrific*, Mark!" she cried, throwing her arms around his neck. "You must be thrilled. One of your own students!"

He shrugged. "I *was* thrilled. I mean, I still am, but it turns out he doesn't want to go."

She stepped back, looking again at the letter in her hand. "Why would he not want to go?"

"Something to do with a summer job. He doesn't want to miss the work."

She shook her head. "Teenagers. I guess money is everything to them."

He took the letter from her and set it on top of the dresser. "I might have thought that about some of the kids I teach, but not Ben. I don't think his family has very much, but he's never said or done anything this year to make me think he'd choose a summer job over something like this."

"Ben Corbett," she said slowly. "You've mentioned him before. Isn't he the one ——"

"Yes, he's the one," he replied. "I thought someone with his ability and interest in writing would jump at the chance to go to this Institute."

She squeezed his hand. "Sometimes we don't know people as well as we think we do," she offered.

"Maybe you're right," he said, slinging the gym bag over his shoulder and following her downstairs. "Maybe you're right."

* * * *

The bottom corner of the glassless storm door scraped against the sagging platform of the back step. It made an arc in the chipped and peeling paint that looked like the smile Ben imagined Shay would be wearing in homeroom the Tuesday after the long weekend. How pathetic he must have looked to Shay as he'd stood on the lawn, clutching blades of grass like a shoplifter with a lump under his jacket. Shay was probably on the phone right now telling people like Alison Myers what had happened. Ben's stomach tightened as he tried to push the memory of those moments from his mind.

Digging in his pockets for his key to the inner door, he looked at the top hinge of the sagging aluminum rectangle and saw it hung by only one screw that had been ripped halfway out of the cracked casing. Another job for Ben to add to his list. But it would have to wait until he finished his regular chores first.

He slid his key into the brass Weiser lock Rankin had installed the day they'd moved into the tiny North Street bungalow. Locks were the only things Rankin ever bought new, and he'd set about replacing the old ones even before Ben and his mother had carried in their first box of belongings. Rankin never told landlords that he changed their locks, but the half-dozen apartments and houses they'd lived in were not the sort of places landlords checked up on anyway. This place was no better than any of the others; in fact, it was worse than most of them. As he'd stood in the rain that first afternoon looking at the sagging roof, cracked chimney, and three colours of vinyl siding that marched unevenly across the front of the house, Ben knew any lock would be unnecessary here: no burglar would give this place a second glance. Of course, locks weren't just for keeping people out.

He unlocked the kitchen door and went in, being careful to take off his sneakers on the mat his mother had braided using rags cut from old shirts and a dress she'd worn the day she and Rankin were married. She'd loved that dress, a simple blue knee-length affair she'd bought secondhand at a thrift shop the day before the ceremony. Ben remembered the way the light had played on the material when his mother moved, remembered the softness of it against his face when he'd clung to her, pleading with her yet again not to marry the man who'd frightened him even then. But most vividly he remembered the sound it had made less than two weeks later as it had torn between Rankin's large hands.

Looking down now at the coils of blue amid the greys and browns of the other rags, Ben thought again about Mr. Lewis's letter and the opportunity it represented, then fought against a helpless rage that began in his belly and had nowhere to go. He saw again the dress tearing between Rankin's hands, except this time the dress was a letter with the words "CANADIAN WRITERS' COUNCIL" in gold script across the top. He saw again Rankin's smile, except this time the smile became a twisted grin, then a snigger, then a gut-wrenching roar. Ben swallowed twice to keep from cursing his stepfather. And, as so often happened when he felt such helplessness, he thought of Ann and longed to be with her, longed to hold her and be held by her while he struggled to keep the anger at bay. He considered calling her — she knew she should never call him, although she'd be anxious to hear what Mr. Lewis had wanted — but he looked at his watch and knew there was no time now. Maybe if he hurried there would be a few minutes before his mother and Rankin got home.

Ben took his books into the tiny bedroom at the

back of the house and set them in the plastic milk crate that doubled as a nightstand when turned on its side. He took off his sweaty shirt and grass-stained jeans, then got fresh clothes out of the cardboard box by his mattress and put them on. In the bathroom he found two plastic Save-Easy bags stuffed with other soiled clothes, and he carried these and his jeans and shirt out to the kitchen. Slipping on his sneakers again, he headed down the narrow stairs to the basement.

Lit by a single forty-watt bulb, the basement was little more than a damp hole in the ground. Although the spring rains had stopped weeks earlier, and the mud outside had dried up, large dark patches on the dirt floor showed where water still seeped in from some underground source. Ben was careful to step only on the boards a former tenant had laid down in runway fashion between the stairs, the oil furnace, and a makeshift laundry area near the far wall.

He emptied the bags onto a broken door laid across two sawhorses, then sorted the light clothes from the dark and put them into an ancient Kenmore washer perched atop four concrete blocks. He took his time arranging the load inside the drum because if the clothes weren't distributed evenly, the Kenmore could walk right off those blocks. That had happened only once before, but Ben had no intention of ever letting it happen again.

Back upstairs, he went to the fridge and took out the two shad Rankin had caught the night before off the old train bridge west of town, then carried them outside to clean. When he had finished, he put the scraps into the metal garbage can beside the step and went back inside, all the while knowing that the rock he put over the lid would not keep out the dogs, cats, and raccoons that roamed North Street after dark. One or more of them would have a meal before the night was over. Nor did Ben mind. He'd have fed them himself if he could. But he couldn't forget what had happened to the mutt he'd made the mistake of feeding in Rockport. After putting the fish into the toaster oven on the narrow Arborite counter, he got two pots out of the bottom cupboard and filled them with water, then went to the fridge again and took out six potatoes and five carrots. Rankin, he knew, would count the remaining vegetables later. Standing at the kitchen sink Ben washed and peeled the vegetables methodically, slicing them into thin pieces that would not take long to cook. As he worked he gazed out the window at Freemont's Lumber Yard across the street, his eyes drawn for the thousandth time to the huge piles of two-by-fours and two-by-sixes stacked everywhere with almost mathematical precision.

The first time he'd seen Freemont's, he'd nearly wept. As bad as the last place they'd lived in had been, there had been a partial view of Rockport's harbour from their apartment in back of Eisner's Ultramar. No matter how rushed he was in the mornings getting ready for school and keeping out of Rankin's way, he would steal a moment to look out at that tiny patch of harbour and watch an unending succession of waves either caress or hammer the breakwater. Ben never tired of that view. There was beauty out there in even the most violent weather.

Here there were only wood chips and soot and mountains of lumber in various shades of grey and tan. Looking out the kitchen window his first day in Brookdale, he'd thought there could be nothing uglier. Now, though, he knew he'd been wrong. Freemont's Lumber Yard wasn't the muscular pulse and roll of the Atlantic Ocean, but even here he'd found something to admire. In the beginning he'd spent his time watching the front-end loaders perform their intricate waltzes between the piles of lumber and the trucks they were loading, wondering where the wood was going and what it might be used to build — homes, businesses, even toolsheds and doghouses, all of them new beginnings of sorts. Then he'd begun to study the order and symmetry of those piles, which were meticulously stacked to allow even airflow around each piece of wood, and he'd marvelled at the patience and skill of the hands that had constructed them. Finally, he'd focused on the truckloads of logs that came into the mill almost daily, most of them spruce and fir leaking sap all over each other. All the logs headed for a huge saw that ripped them first into slabs and then smaller blades sliced them into the various stock sizes that dried outside in the yard. Ben listened to the mill's whine and chatter that went on every day except Sunday, and he admired how wood that had been savaged by saws could emerge smooth and useful, as if this was its destiny.

It was this ability to look at things in reverse that had surprised and impressed Ben's teachers in each of the schools he'd attended. Although they found him quiet and withdrawn, he did well in school because he was able to look beyond the brick wall that was the math problem, the essay topic, or the test question to see the options holding the secret to its solution. Mr. Lewis had seen this same ability reflected in Ben's writing — his ability, as the teacher had put it, to study people and situations and to notice details that most individuals overlooked. Like the strange beauty in Freemont's Lumber Yard that Ben himself had overlooked until he'd taken the time to really see it. In fact, his observations of the mill became the prose poem "Walking Backwards" that he had written for Mr. Lewis. And for himself.

Ben thought again of the comment he'd read in the letter from the Canadian Writers' Council. "Damn," he whispered, his fingers fiercely gripping the potato he was peeling. If only there was a way.

Suddenly there was a burning sensation and a moment of release, and he looked down to see red threads swirling among the white vegetables. "DAMN!" he hissed, popping his index finger into his mouth and heading down the narrow hallway to the bathroom. The cracked mirror of the tiny medicine cabinet reflected two right hands as he opened the door. Inside was a Super Economy Size ("Now you won't run out") carton of no-name bandages, but it was empty. Ben crumpled it in his free hand and flung it against the bathroom wall, the coppery taste of blood and anger filling his mouth. He stood for a long moment looking at the crumpled box like a white fist against the scarred linoleum; then, sighing, he picked it up and carried it out to the garbage can beneath the kitchen sink.

Also under the sink were rags Ben's mother used for cleaning, and he reached in and pulled one out. Lifting the pots out of the sink, he turned the faucet on and stuck his finger under its cool pressure, watching the flap of skin open like a book and run red. At the same time, he gripped one end of the rag between his teeth and pulled the other end with his good right hand, tearing a strip from the cloth. Turning off the water, he dried his finger on one end, then wrapped the strip around it three times and managed to tie both ends in a knot. A red stain flowered faintly in the middle of the cloth but grew no larger.

Peeling the rest of the vegetables was a painful process, but he had only himself to blame. He'd broken his own rule: Be Alert. Years ago in a post office he'd seen a "Crime Stoppers" poster with the words "BE ALERT" printed in fat red letters across the top, below which someone had scrawled, "The world needs more lerts." Ben knew the value of being alert. But you had to be able to do more than read a poster. You had to be able to read the signs. The danger signals. You could never let your guard down, not even for a moment. Or you'd live to regret it.

Once the vegetables were cooking on the hot plate, Ben went to the kitchen closet and took out Rankin's toolbox, the only thing belonging to his stepfather that Rankin let him touch. Over the years Ben had had lots of opportunity to use the tools it contained, and today he got out a hammer and a Phillips screwdriver. Going out on the back step, he looked at the storm door again, assessing the damage. Fortunately there was no glass to clean up — the window had been broken the week before Christmas, when Ben's mother had come home late from work. Irene, the head cashier at Save-Easy, had twisted her ankle on the ice and they'd needed someone to cover for her because of the holiday rush. Ben had stayed late at school to work on a research assignment he'd wanted to pass in before the holidays started, and his mother hadn't been able to reach him. Supper wasn't on the table at 5:30. And, as Rankin later ranted, hadn't they been warned? On her knees amid blood and broken glass, Ben's mother admitted they had.

Luckily, the door was still square — when Ben pushed the hinge against the casing, the door swung freely without scraping the step. Small mercies, Ben thought. He removed the screw and hammered the kink out of the hinge plate, then re-screwed it to the casing a little left of the crack.

When he opened and closed the door again, it squeaked a bit but swung true.

"Good job, Ben."

Ben whirled about to see his mother standing at the foot of the step with a full Save-Easy bag dangling from each hand. He had no idea how long she'd been watching him, and he felt vulnerable. That was the second time that day he'd failed to Be Alert. No, the third if you counted what had happened that afternoon in the Heights. He thought again of Mr. Lewis's letter and the effect it had had on him. *Let it go,* he told himself. *Just let it go.*

"Thanks," he said, jumping off the step and taking the bags from her. "What've you got here?" He opened one of them and saw bananas with black edges.

"Mr. Wile was going to throw them out. Too many came in on the Tuesday truck and they weren't selling fast enough, even at half off." She sat down on the bottom step and slipped off her sneakers. "He didn't want to keep them over the long weekend, so I asked if I could have a few." She pulled one foot up over her knee and massaged her sole, kneading and rubbing it with both hands.

"Did you have to ask?" Ben looked over her head at the door he'd just fixed.

"They were headed for the dumpster, Ben." A moment passed. "I'm not the only clerk to ask for food," she added softly.

He doubted that but wanted to change the subject. "There's a lot here. What do you plan to do with them all?" he asked.

"We'll have some for dessert tonight, with milk. And I'm going to make some banana breads after supper. The church is having a bake sale tomorrow to raise money for the missionary society, and I think I have enough bananas to make at least four loaves for the sale and one for Sadie. She said I could use her oven and she'll throw in the sugar and flour."

Ben looked across at the only other house on this end of North Street, a tiny bungalow with three wooden butterflies nailed above the front door. Its owner, Sadie Jackson, was eighty-something and belonged to the same church as his mother — had, in fact, come to call with apple crisp the day after they'd moved in and invited the whole family to come to church with her the following Sunday. Although stooped and twisted with arthritis, Sadie walked the three and a half blocks to the Brookdale Baptist Church every Sunday as though leading a parade. After all, she hadn't missed a worship service since Pearson was prime minister.

Ben liked Sadie. He had declined her invitation to church — as had his stepfather — but not her later invitations to sit on her step or in her kitchen rocking chair where she served him diet Coke, the second of her two addictions. The first, of course, was Jesus Christ.

Sadie was the first black person Ben had ever gotten to know. There had been black kids in some of his classes over the years, but he'd never made friends with them — or with any of his other classmates, either. In fact, Sadie was his first real friend. Even before Ann. Ben was often surprised at how much Sadie and he had in common: she'd grown up with no brothers or sisters, raised by an elderly aunt in New Brunswick; she'd moved eleven times following her husband, Franklin, who worked on the railway and died the year before his retirement when a coupling let go and a flatcar rolled back on him; and she wrote poetry in spidery letters that seemed to crawl off the page right into his heart.

Ben was even more surprised that Rankin allowed him this friendship; from time to time his stepfather would make a crack about his visits with Sadie, and Ben would wait for the decree to end all contact with her, but it never came. At least, not yet. Perhaps it was because Sadie made the best apple crisp in the province ("Better'n a bakery," Rankin once mumbled with his mouth full). More likely, though, it was because she was nearly deaf. Batteries were expensive, and Sadie only ever turned on her hearing aid during Sunday services, *Another World,* and those occasions when someone came to call. Ben often wondered what it must be like to be able to shut off the world with the touch of a button.

Off in the distance, the church carillon chimed the first two bars of "Amazing Grace," reminding the town it was 5:15. Ben's eyes met his mother's and he saw in them the same flicker of fear that appeared there every workday afternoon before Rankin arrived home. He knew that fear intimately; they both had lived with it for seven years. It was the fear of never knowing what to expect. Sometimes Rankin came home smiling and laughing, telling coarse jokes he'd heard at the elastic plant in Centrefield where he worked. Other times he was sullen and uncommunicative and would sit at the table and stare across the room at nothing while he chewed the food that didn't end up on his face or the floor. And then there were those times when they would hear him coming a block away, the bald tires on his old Ford LTD squealing as he flung the car down North Street and screeched into the gravel driveway. Even before he slammed the rust-spotted door, they would know it was going to be bad.

Amazingly, though, it was the first of these arrivals that Ben dreaded most. The others, at least, provided some warning, making him weigh his every word and movement and consider the effect each might have on his stepfather. It was when Rankin was most cheerful that he was most dangerous, the whip-like rage appearing without warning. Like the night shortly after Rankin had married Ben's mother. They'd all been sitting at the supper table laughing about something when suddenly his mother was on the floor, her nose running red, Rankin standing over her roaring "What the hell are you laughing at?" Ben had thought his mother was dying — it was the first time he had seen her bleed.

"Is supper ready?" his mother asked, her eyes travelling the length of North Street to Main.

"Just about," Ben said.

Standing up, she removed the pin that kept her hair in a bun on those days she worked and she shook her head from side to side. Thick, dark waves fell about her face, reminding Ben of the photograph he'd taped back together and hidden under his mattress. It was a picture of his mother when she wasn't much older than Ben was now. She was sitting on a hillside blanketed with dandelions, a porcelain sky reflecting the blue of her enormous eyes. Her hair was blowing about her face but did not hide the smile — almost a laugh — the camera had caught as she'd turned towards it. Ben had risked reprisal when he'd retrieved that photograph from the trash, one of only three that hadn't been mutilated completely, but it had been worth it. There tucked safely under his mattress was evidence that his mother once could smile. But it was also evidence of another kind. The few times Ben dared take out the picture to look at it, he'd found himself thinking less about the wonder of that smile than about the existence of the person who had shared it, perhaps initiated it. The person who had held the camera. Ben's father.

Ben watched his mother pick up her sneakers and climb the steps, moving stiffly as she often did after standing long hours behind a cash register, and he thought about the murder of that girl in the photograph taken so long ago. Of course no court would call it that, but it was definitely murder. There was, after all, more than one kind of dying. Some dead people were just difficult to spot, moving their bodies around in a semblance of living.

The aroma of boiled vegetables and baked fish should have reminded Ben that he hadn't eaten since breakfast but, watching his mother scurry about the tiny kitchen setting the table while he poured water into gas station glasses that didn't match, he was aware only of the urgency of her movements. When she turned quickly and nearly knocked one of the glasses from his hand, Ben said softly, "Hey, slow down."

His mother looked at him and turned the corners of her mouth up but there was only that flicker in her eyes. "He'll be here soon," she said, her voice almost a whisper.

Ben stood back and let her pass. She took the pots off the hot plate and drained them, then took a masher from the single drawer and began squashing the potatoes until their white meat oozed rectangular prisms through the stainless steel grid. He noticed she mashed with her left hand, and he knew her right shoulder — the shoulder that had struck the corner of the table when Rankin had knocked her to the floor the previous night — must hurt even more than he suspected. In the basement the washer was in its final spin, the whir like a drill through Ben's brain.

"Why do you let him do it?"

He was surprised he'd said it. It was almost as if

another person had entered the room and spoken for him. Surely he could not have asked such a question.

His mother stopped in midmash and turned to him. "Let who do what?" she asked, but he could tell she knew what he meant. Turning back to the pot, she said, "He didn't mean to. Really." And then, more softly, "Things will get better soon. You'll see."

He couldn't put the cat back into the bag. It was out now and moving around, its long body weaving in and out between their legs. "Things are not going to change. *He's* not going to change."

"Yes, he will," she said, her eyes fastened on the contents of the pot, which, by now, looked more like pudding than potatoes. "I like my spuds whipped," Rankin was fond of saying, and repeated mashing was the only alternative to the electric mixer they couldn't afford.

Ben's anger came from nowhere and everywhere, from an envelope with fancy lettering, from a lawn that looked like carpet, from a door that would take perhaps one more smash against the side of the house before it was damaged beyond repair. "How can you say that? How can you go on believing that at some point he has to stop?"

Her reply was so soft that Ben had to strain to hear it above the whir of the washer beneath their feet. "You have to have faith, Ben."

"Faith?" He almost spat the word as he fought

to control his voice and the tremor in his face. "What the hell is that?"

She took a knife from the drawer and scraped back into the pot the potato that clung to the metal masher. Nothing was wasted. "Ben, the Bible says that faith is the assurance of things hoped for, the conviction of things not seen. I *know* things will get better. You have to believe it, too."

Ben had to swallow to keep from choking, to keep from screaming. "Don't quote scripture to me! I believe, all right. I believe that one day Rankin's going to want to kill you or me and there's nothing we'll be able to do about it!"

"Ben, please." She glanced out the door and down the street. "He'll be here any minute."

"I don't care. I'm sick of what he's done to us. Look at you. Is this all you want out of life? To be a punching bag?"

Her anger surprised him. "Of course it's not what I want! How can you think that? I do the best I can. We haven't always had a roof over our heads, or have you forgotten? At least we have clothes on our backs and food in our stomachs. What do you think is out there for us that's any better? I went as far in school as you are right now. I'm lucky to have the job I have. And your step-father is lucky to have the job *he* has." She paused for a moment, as if searching for words. The washer thunked, then slowed to a stop. "No, things aren't perfect. But the world isn't perfect either. We do the best we can with what we have. We just have to try harder."

"*We* aren't the problem here! Don't you see

that? You just said you're doing the best you can. *I'm* doing the best *I* can." His words caught in his throat like half-chewed meat and he wiped the back of his sleeve savagely across his eyes, ashamed of the tears that brimmed them.

She moved towards him and put her left hand on his shoulder and her face next to his. "I know you are, Benjamin. I don't know what I'd do without you." She paused, her forehead touching his. It felt strangely cool in the stuffy kitchen. "I would take it all if I could."

He knew what she meant and clung to her. It was worse when they stood up for each other, like waving a flag in a bull pen. It was better to stand back so there'd be someone left to pick up the pieces later. But Ben had seen his mother's face behind Rankin's raised hands, clenched fists, and he knew every blow that found his head or belly or back connected also with some fragile part inside her. "I know," he said. "I know."

In the distance the carillon chimed again, and Ben listened as his mother sang softly, "Amazing Grace, how sweet the sound, that saved a wretch like me —"

Then Rankin's old LTD barrelled into the driveway.

4

Ben was careful not to watch his stepfather eat, but he could not ignore the sounds the man made as he shovelled food into his mouth. They were the only sounds in the kitchen. Ben and his mother had already finished eating.

Ben missed the ticking of the windup clock that used to sit on top of the old refrigerator. Often he had spent his suppers counting the ticks, once getting as high as 739. He'd written about that clock in a poem he'd never shown Mr. Lewis, referring to his counting as "the measure of my normality." He'd nearly convinced himself that if he could get to 1,000 everything would finally be all right. Now he would never know.

"Would you like some more bananas, Jim?"

Ben's mother asked.

Rankin grunted no, then pushed his chair back from the table. "Good supper," he said, then stood up, his six-foot-four frame seeming to fill the room. He was thickening around the middle, but his shoulders and upper arms could have belonged to a man half his age.

"Ben got it ready," his mother said quietly as she and Ben got up to clear the table. As she moved around her husband to get his dishes, he reached out and grabbed her about the waist, pulling her towards him. For a second she cowered, reminding Ben of the dog his stepfather had "got rid of" in Rockport; then, as he hugged her against his barrel-like chest, she relaxed. "Jim," she whispered, "not in front of Ben."

Putting his face in her hair, he murmured, "Ahh, Ben's a big boy. He knows all about the birds 'n' the bees. Don'tcha, Ben?"

Putting his plate and glass in the sink, Ben felt the fish in his stomach move and he looked away. "I know," he said simply.

Rankin inhaled deeply. "You smell nice," he told his wife.

"Rayeanne at work was showing us a new perfume she bought, and she sprayed some on me during our break," she said. Her tone suggested she meant to sound annoyed at the prank, but Ben could tell that she was touched by her husband's compliment. Ben turned on the faucet and concentrated on the water that slowly covered the dishes.

Rankin put his hands on his wife's bottom and pulled her closer, squeezing her even tighter in his big arms. For a moment they looked like any other husband and wife still in love after seven years of marriage. But then Ben's mother gasped, and he knew Rankin's arms had found her bruised shoulder. Ben poured liquid detergent into the sink and watched a handful of bubbles struggle to life in the hard water.

Rankin released her. "Hurt?" he asked, and Ben turned to see something like concern on his face.

"Mmm," his mother said, her eyes sliding floorward.

Rankin looked at her carefully. "You know I didn't mean it," he said. He could have been talking about misplacing car keys.

"I know," Ben's mother said softly. She glanced at Ben, but Ben turned to the sink again. Shutting off the hot water, he added some cold.

The moment had passed. Rankin cleared his throat and moved away from his wife. In a single stride he was at the doorway. "Back later," he said.

"When?" The word was spoken softly, a spiderweb in the air. Even she appeared surprised she'd said it.

Rankin seemed not to hear. He walked out on the back step, pausing momentarily to look at the repairs Ben had made to the storm door, then headed down the stairs and across the gravel to the car. The Ford started on the third try and he backed out and headed towards downtown. Ben knew where he was going. So did his mother.

The two of them finished clearing the table, working in silence — almost as though each was alone in the room. It was a pattern they'd fallen into years earlier when they'd learned that Rankin didn't like a lot of talking. "Talk's for politicians and do-nothin's," he'd said. And, as far as he was concerned, books were "just talk written down." Ben had learned early on to hide whatever he might be reading or writing. The only books that were safe in their house were those he brought home from school — even Rankin wouldn't destroy something he'd have to pay good money to replace.

Ben glanced sideways at his mother and saw the lines on her forehead and around her eyes, the grey hair beginning to show at her temple, the way she favoured her right arm to ease the soreness in her shoulder. He tried again to see the girl in the photograph and failed. He put his hand on her arm. "I'll do these. Why don't you sit down?"

She looked up from the counter she was wiping and put her free hand over his, giving it a gentle squeeze. "Thanks, Ben. Actually, what I'd like to do is take these bananas over to Sadie's and get started on those breads. Do you mind?" She glanced down at the rag tied around his finger. She had not asked him about it. That, too, was part of the pattern of their lives.

He shook his head. "Go on. It'll only take me a minute to finish up here."

She took off her apron and folded it neatly over the back of one of the wooden chairs Rankin had picked up at a yard sale in Rockport. It had once been part of a set of four, but only three remained. Ben didn't know what had happened to the other one. One day it was there and the next it wasn't. "What do you plan to do this evening?" she asked, reaching for the bags of bananas on the counter.

"Nothing. Maybe walk uptown and hang out," he lied. He'd never hung out in his life, something he was sure his mother suspected. Most often he went to the library. It was quiet there, and he could have any book on the shelves for free. More important, it was a place he and Ann could meet where Rankin would never see them.

"The Young People's group is meeting tonight at the church. Maybe you'd like to go."

"I don't think so," Ben said, rinsing a plate under the faucet.

She pressed on. "There are some nice kids in it. They help out at church functions all the time. You may even know some of them. One of them is named Lisa. Her mother works at the drugstore. I know you've seen her around."

"Lisa Benedict," he said. "She's in my math class."

"There you are, Ben, someone you know. What do you think? Will you go?"

Ben could not believe he was hearing this, not after the last time. "No," he said quietly.

His mother stood looking at his back for a moment, then turned and got a sweater off the hook by the door and put it on. "Ben," she said softly, "things are better now. We have a life here."

He didn't turn around. "You're the one with all the faith. Not me."

He heard the door close behind her and listened to her footsteps down the wooden stairs and across the gravel driveway. Even when they'd faded away he still stood listening, as if trying to hear a memory.

* * * *

He'd known from the beginning it was a mistake to go away on that weekend outing with the Rockport Teens for Christ. Even when his mother first told him about it, he knew she wasn't thinking clearly. She'd seen it as a chance for him to be with other people his own age, ordinary people who laughed and played games and didn't spend every waking hour looking over their shoulders. And it was a chance for him to spend time with adults like Peter and Moira MacIssac, the young assistant pastor and his wife whose energy and enthusiasm had tripled the size of the youth group in the year they'd been with the church. All the kids liked Pastor Pete and Moira, including Ben who, at his mother's urging, had attended two of the group's evening get-togethers. But a weekend was something else. It would be easy to make a mistake.

Ben never knew what his mother had done to convince Rankin to let him go. He wasn't even sure what she had said to convince himself to go.

He didn't share his mother's love for the church and had stopped going to Sunday service with his mother when he was eleven.

But there he was standing in the church vestry waiting for the last youth group member to arrive, and he'd felt strangely free. He barely knew the other kids and was tongue-tied and awkward around them, especially the girls, but Pastor Pete raced about the group like a dervish entertaining everyone with his funny stories and practical jokes so that even Ben felt included. His sides ached from laughing by the time the church vans pulled up in front of the ragtag collection of cabins that Rockport Baptists called their retreat.

That first night was the best of Ben's life. They'd all sat around a campfire roasting wieners and singing songs, the lake behind them a vast black bowl cradling the moon and the Milky Way. Then the ghost stories started, and before he knew it, Ben was first telling one he had read, then two more he made up on the spot. The others had listened with delight as he created worlds filled with fantastic creatures who preyed on unsuspecting victims, and when it was time to turn in they made him promise to tell more the following night.

Lying in his bunk that evening, he had felt for the first time as if he was part of something other than what remained behind in Rockport. It was a good feeling, one he wouldn't let go, and he lay awake far into the night listening to the loons make their eerie music out on that black water.

Although it was mid-September, the next morning dawned bright and hot as if to prove it was, after all, officially still summer for two more days. Most people had packed only jeans and long-sleeved shirts, and by the time Pastor Pete led the group through a full morning of hiking and exploring, everyone was sweltering. After lunch someone suggested they all go for a swim, and it wasn't long before Peter and Moira found in the main cabin enough old shorts, trunks, and swimsuits for everyone.

Ben declined the offer of the swimming trunks. "I'll just sit up here on the verandah and watch," he said. The others tried to coax him but he was determined, and soon they were in the lake while he remained on the sagging deck that wrapped around all four sides of the main cabin.

He sat there for half an hour watching the group shriek and splash about in the cold water, imagining the feel of it against his sweat-drenched body. Then Peter came back up from the lake with three of the boys, water streaming off their bodies onto the verandah. "Come on, Ben," the pastor said, "it's cold but it feels great." To prove the point he shook his head over him, showering him with icy droplets.

Ben smiled nervously and shook his head. "No, thanks. I'm fine here."

But Peter MacIssac would not be refused. "Ben, swimming is anything but a spectator sport." And suddenly all four were carrying him down the path to the water's edge, the rest of the group chanting his name: "Ben, Ben, Ben, Ben."

The water did feel good, but not as good as the sound of his name in their voices, the sound of acquaintances who had become friends in the span of a day. He thrashed about in the freezing water making a complete spectacle of himself and thoroughly enjoying it while the others cheered him on. Even the weight of his wet clothes did not encumber him, so buoyant was his joy. Months later he would write about the experience being like a baptism that made him feel fresh and new inside.

When they came out of the water, everyone headed up to the cabins to change. Ben lagged behind the others, pretending to look for a comb he held hidden in his hand until he was sure the boys in his cabin had finished dressing. When they had all come out, he went in and stripped his clothes off as quickly as he could, then pulled on clean underwear and a dry pair of jeans. He was just pulling a long-sleeved sweatshirt over his head when the door opened and Pastor Pete's voice said, "Ben, we're ready to —"

Ben jerked the sweatshirt down his back, but not fast enough. He turned, and he could read it in the pastor's face. He had seen.

"I'll be there in a minute," Ben said, but he could feel his heart hammering against his ribs. He bent down to pick up his wet clothes.

"Ben?"

"Yes, sir?" Ben continued to rummage around the floor.

"What happened to your back?"

"Nothing. I just fell."

"Look at me, Ben."

Ben stood up slowly, his eyes still on the floor.

"Ben?"

Ben looked up at the pastor's face. It was open and safe.

Peter stepped inside the cabin and closed the door behind him. "Tell me what happened." His voice was quiet and steady, but Ben could hear something turbid in it, like he needed to swallow but couldn't.

"I fell," Ben repeated.

The pastor didn't say anything for a long moment. Then, "When?"

Although the uninsulated cabin was oven-hot, Ben felt an icy chill wash over him. *I knew I shouldn't have come. Why did I come?* "Last week. I was standing on a chair changing a lightbulb and I lost my balance." *I shouldn't have come.*

"Did you see a doctor about it?"

"No. Really, it looks worse than it is." *Shouldn't have come.*

"What it looks like is a footprint." The pastor moved across the room and stood beside Ben. "Are you telling me the truth, Ben?"

Shouldn't! "Yes," he said, clenching his teeth together to keep them from chattering. He was so cold.

Peter raised his hand, intending to lay it on Ben's shoulder, but Ben flinched and stepped back. The pastor let his hand fall to his side and studied the boy's white face. "Ben," he said slowly, carefully, "I can help you. There are all kinds of people who can help you. You don't have to take that. No one deserves that sort of treatment."

SHOULDN'TSHOULDN'TSHOULDN'T! "I don't need any help. I fell. Why won't you believe me? I fell!"

Outside the cabin a locust zeeeeeeeeed. A chipmunk sauced, then exploded in an endless stream of chatter. A crow cawed raucously from a nearby treetop. And, from down by the lake, fifteen voices called, "Pastor PEEEEEEEEEEeeeeet! We're WAAAAAAAAAITing!"

The pastor studied Ben's face for another moment, then shook his head. Turning back to the door, he said, "We're going to take the canoes out and it sounds like the natives are restless. Don't be long, okay?"

"No, sir." But, watching out the window, Ben waited until the pastor had reached the others before he left the cabin.

* * * *

Looking out the window over the kitchen sink, Ben couldn't recall much of what had happened the rest of that weekend. He remembered only the shame he'd felt as he tried to avoid Peter MacIssac the rest of that afternoon, feigned a headache to miss the campfire, hurried thefollowing morning to get a seat in the van that Moira MacIssac was driving back to Rockport. The return trip was interminable and, when Moira dropped him in front of Eisner's Ultramar, he couldn't get out of the van fast enough, almost tripping over the bag that contained his still-wet clothes. He couldn't even remember if he'd said thank you.

What he remembered vividly was the following night when Rankin got home late from work. It was nearly six o'clock before the kitchen door swung open, slamming back against the counter and making the dishes rattle. Both Ben and his mother had been waiting at the table, their scalloped potatoes untouched, but both had jumped guiltily. Ben's mother had gotten up and taken Rankin's lunch box from him and pulled his chair out from the table, but he'd continued to stand in the doorway staring at Ben for a few seconds before finally sitting down.

Then he'd been pleasant and talkative, telling them about Bob Walker at the fish plant who had won nearly five thousand dollars in the lottery. He'd told them that Linda Bezanson, the secretary in the office, had just given birth to twin girls. Then he'd told them they were moving to Brookdale.

And Ben had made the mistake of saying he wouldn't go. Ignoring the voice in his head screaming *SHUT UP! SHUT UP!*, he'd said he wouldn't move again so soon. He wouldn't.

There had been a long moment of silence during which Rankin studied his potatoes and Ben tried to swallow, tried to breathe. Another moment passed. Then, just as Ben raised his glass to drink, his stepfather's hand struck him.

Ben's mother had screamed even before Ben knew what had happened, before he realized he was on the floor, his chair on top of him, broken glass everywhere. She had still been screaming when Rankin pushed her out the door and locked it, shouting at her through the window to shut up if she knew what was good for both of them. Then he'd grabbed Ben by his bloody shirt and yanked him up on his toes, all the while yelling about Peter MacIssac waiting for him in the plant parking lot when he'd gotten off work. He'd told Ben — at the top of his lungs, his spit flying in Ben's face — what it was like "to have a runt like that threaten me with the police if I ever laid a hand on you again." And then he'd lowered his voice and growled, "If you ever say anythin' to anybody again, I'll kill you."

Only then did Rankin unlock the door and let Ben's mother take him to Outpatients.

Ben reached up and touched his forehead, feeling with his fingertips the raised semicircle that was an emblem of his foolishness. He would never make the same mistake again. Never.

Just then the telephone on the wall by the fridge jangled and he picked up the receiver before it could ring again. "Hello?"

"Ben?"

His heart skipped a beat. "Ann? What's wrong?"

"Nothing. I know I'm not supposed to call but I couldn't wait any longer. I was wondering what Mr. Lewis wanted. Will I see you tonight?"

Now Ben could breathe again. "You're right. You're never supposed to call here," he said, his voice low. "I can't talk now. Meet you in about ten minutes?"

"Okay. And, Ben?"

"Yes?"

"I was so proud of you today in class. Your story was wonderful."

Ben flushed and his heart did a lazy roll in his chest. "Thanks, Ann. See you in a bit, all right?"

"I'll be there."

He heard the receiver on the other end of the line bump against plastic. "Ann?" he said quickly.

"Yes?"

"I love you."

He could see her face as she said it. "I love you, too, Ben."

He hung up the receiver and turned to see Rankin looking at him through the kitchen door.

5

"Who was that on the phone?" Rankin asked as he opened the door. He carried a two-four of Moosehead beer under his arm and there was grease on his shirtsleeves that had not been there at supper.

Ben shrugged his shoulders and tried to appear indifferent while his mind clamoured, *Didhehear? Didhehear?* "A girl looking for an Adam something-or-other." He was surprised at how easily the lie came. How many lies had he told that day?

Rankin looked at him with narrowed eyes, then came into the kitchen leaving the door open behind him. A fly buzzed in and bumbled about the tiny room and flew out again. He set the case of beer on the table, then opened it and took out one of the long-necked brown bottles. He twisted the cap off in his hand and some of the warm liquid fizzed out and onto the floor. Putting the bottle to his lips, he drained it in a half-dozen noisy swallows. He belched — the sound somehow seal-like — and wiped the back of his hand across his mouth, then opened another bottle and drank half of that.

Ben wondered why he hadn't heard his step-father come back — *BE ALERT,* he thought again — and glanced out the open door. The LTD was nowhere to be seen. "Where's the car?" he asked.

Rankin narrowed his eyes again and Ben felt his stepfather look straight through him. When would he learn to keep his mouth shut? The thought of seeing Ann had made him careless.

"She quit on me," Rankin said finally, then drained the rest of the second bottle. "Over on Commercial. I need you to push." He took six more bottles out of the box and set them in the fridge, then turned to the door again. "You comin'?" He glanced at the telephone and a twisted smile played on his lips. "That is, as long as you 'n' Adam something-or-other ain't got plans."

Ben flushed and bent down to put on his sneakers, not bothering to tie the laces but shoving them inside. He thought of Ann, who would be waiting at the library, and silently cursed his luck. As they left, Rankin locked the door behind him, the brass bolt of the Weiser sliding deep into the cracked wooden casing.

* * * *

More than an hour later, he found her waiting outside the old rambling one-storey building, her feet dangling over the side of the brick step. Behind her, the "CLOSED" sign hung inside the glass door, one end lower than the other reminding Ben of Rankin's crooked smile.

"I'm sorry, Ann," he said, wrapping his arms around her when she'd stood and come down the steps to meet him. "His car broke down and I had to help him push it to Cruikshank's." Ben's face still burned at the memory of horns honking as cars cruised past, most of them driven by Friday-night teenagers laughing at the sight of someone else's misfortune. He had imagined Shay Phillips behind much of that laughter and had lowered his head and pressed his shoulder even harder against the trunk of the old Ford. Rankin, though, had smiled and waved back, a heck of a good guy having a really bad day. But Ben knew the price of that good humour.

Miraculously, his stepfather had been too tired to make him pay that price. When they got home from Cruikshank's Irving Station, Rankin had popped two more beer and sat in the living room in front of the black-and-white television he'd bought at a yard sale for eight dollars. He'd been asleep in seconds.

"Hey, no problem," Ann said into Ben's shirt. "I was just afraid my phone call had set him off."

Neither of them had spoken Rankin's name, yet

it was as though he were there beside them, behind them, a constant presence. Ben had heard the tremor in Ann's voice and he held her even tighter. Her hair smelled like peaches, the same smell he'd noticed about her the first night they'd met. It had been the previous October right here at the Brookdale Library, formerly the Brookdale Elementary School until the provincial government had built the new primary-to-six facility on Marshall Street and the school board had sold the old building to the town for a dollar.

It had been an open meeting of the Western Valley Writers' Society (WVWS) held nearly a year after Ben and his family had moved to Brookdale. Someone had put up a hand-lettered poster in the library advertising the event, and Ben had read it countless times: "The WVWS invites the public to attend its annual fall Harvest of the Heart, an evening of readings by and dialogue with local writers." Ben had been amazed by the idea that people could read aloud what they'd written to an unknown audience, could expose their thoughts and their feelings for complete strangers to scrutinize. He'd been sharing his writing for over a month in Mr. Lewis's English class, but in small groups and only because the teacher required it. He couldn't imagine anyone wanting to do the same thing in public, but it was something he longed to see. And because Rankin was working the three-to-eleven shift that week at the elastic plant, he did.

He'd been disappointed by the event, which

attracted only a dozen or so nonmembers —
halfway through the evening he'd silently
renamed it Harvest of the Humdrum. Most of the
writers were middle-aged or older, men and
women with more time on their hands than
talent, and he had been embarrassed for several of
them as he'd listened to their halting, self-
conscious voices read excerpts of flowery narra-
tives and sentimental poetry typical of greeting
cards. He admired the courage they exhibited in
their willingness to share their writing and listen
to responses, but by the beginning of the second
hour he'd begun imagining ways he could leave
without appearing rude. He'd almost decided to
fake a coughing spell when the door of the
Reading Room opened and a girl about Ben's age
entered and sat in the chair at the end of his row.

He couldn't take his eyes off her. A slight girl
with fawn-coloured hair, she wore a jean jacket
over a green turtleneck, a long flowered skirt, and
heavy black hiking boots she could only have
bought from a wilderness outfitter. She had the
largest eyes of anyone he'd ever seen, and she'd
kept them focused straight ahead while the readings continued. In her hand was a piece of paper
rolled into a thin cylinder, and from time to time
she unrolled it and smoothed it between her
hands, then re-rolled it even more tightly. At first
Ben thought it was a programme like the one he'd
picked up at the librarian's desk when he'd
arrived, but soon he realized she, too, had written
something she wanted to share. During the last

minutes of the Harvest, he had willed her to unroll it again, silently encouraging her to do what he could never do himself, and when the society's chairman asked a final time if there were any nonmembers who wanted to read, Ben had looked at her and held his breath.

She'd put up her hand at the very last moment, then looked at it wide-eyed as if surprised to see it in the air. All eyes on her as she stood at the front of the room, she'd read as though she, too, had been holding her breath. She wore braces and her words often had the soft edges those metal wires created, but it wasn't her voice that had struck Ben — it was the way her words painted portraits on the insides of his eyes. She read three poems, each of them cryptic and evocative, but the last one left Ben reeling. Listening to it, he felt like she'd opened up his head and taken a long look inside, then written down his entire life in a few lines:

> *Free fall artist*
> *out of touch with myself*
> *nothing but space*
> *and elongated illusion rushing past,*
> *cold fingers clawing my face clutching*
> *emptiness and me.*
> *"Christ, I'm tired!"*
> *Of pretence*
> *like parachute strings*
> *holding me up*
> *while letting me down.*

When she'd finished he had sat there silent, seemingly indifferent, not hearing the responses of the chairman and the other members of the society who thanked her for sharing. He had been numb with the knowledge that, for the first time, he had found someone who knew exactly what it was like to be Ben Corbett.

Minutes later when the meeting broke up, he watched her leave the Reading Room and then hurried after her. He had no idea what he was doing or what he would say to her. He only knew he had to say something, had to tell her how deeply her poetry had moved him.

When he'd pushed open the glass door, she was already moving down the walkway in front of the library, the autumn darkness enveloping her like black water. "Excuse me," he called after her but she'd hurried on, intent only on getting where she was going. "Excuse me," he called again, and this time she paused and looked back over her shoulder.

Ben came down the brick steps and walked towards her, wondering at each footstep how foolish he must appear, yet marvelling that he was indeed putting one foot in front of the other, walking towards a stranger instead of away. For a moment he almost turned back to the library, then thought again of her poems and the effect they'd had on him.

"Hi," he said, then swallowed. He could hear the sound in his throat like soft fruit gripped by a fist, and he cursed his shyness.

"Hi," she said. She'd turned completely around

and he saw her paper again curled tube-like in her hand.

"I wanted to tell you —" he began and then lost himself in those enormous eyes.

"Yes?" she asked after a moment. (Later, Ben would wonder how long he'd have stood there if she hadn't spoken.)

"My name's Ben," he said quickly and he held out his hand.

"I'm Ann," she said, giving him hers. It was the one with the paper in it and his hand closed over her poems. "Sorry," she said, switching the paper to her other hand and extending the first one again. "I'm a little rattled."

Her hand felt like warm silk and he fought an urge to tighten his, to enfold hers with fingers unaccustomed to another's touch. The smell of peaches swirled about him in the cool night air and he inhaled deeply, forcing the fragrance deeper into his lungs. For a moment he felt intoxicated, then remembered it was his turn to speak. "Rattled?" he echoed, releasing her hand. Reluctantly.

She nodded. "I made a bet with myself," she said. "I almost lost." For a moment he thought she'd spoken his name, then realized what she'd said. "Bet?" he echoed again, then cringed at how parrot-like he sounded.

She shrugged her shoulders. "Nothing, really. I was at a meeting in the library. I'm just coming from there."

Amazingly, she hadn't seen him. "I know," he

said. "I was there, too."

Her eyes widened and in the pale wash of the streetlight Ben could just make out a pink flush that rose from her throat to her cheeks. "Really? I came late." She looked down at the paper in her hand and Ben thought he could hear her swallow, too. "Did you read?"

"No," he assured her, almost smiling at the absurdity of her question.

She looked up at him. "Are you a member?"

This time he did smile. "No," he explained. "I don't think they let anyone under sixty join."

She laughed, the sound a bright yellow bird in the darkness. "I think you're right. I've never seen so many bifocals in one place."

And then he was laughing too, their voices intertwined like ivy on a stone wall. Ben listened to the sound float up into the night, amazed that he had taken part in its making.

The library door opened behind them and four people came out, moving down the steps and across the walkway towards them. The group split in two as it passed them, then became one again on the other side.

"I guess we're in the way," she said.

"I guess we are." He could think of nothing else to say.

A moment passed. Then the library door opened again as others began to leave.

"I should be going," she said. "It was nice to meet you, Ben." And then she turned.

"Ann?"

"Yes?" she'd said, looking back over her shoulder while still moving away.

"I wanted to tell you —"

She'd stopped, her face a white carnation suspended in ink. "Tell me what?"

And then it had come all at once, a headlong rush over the falls. "Your poems. They were the best things read in there tonight. All three of them. But especially the last one. When you finished reading it I was shaking. I'm shaking now." And he was. His whole body was trembling. He suddenly recalled his last memory of Rockport, a wet cat huddled against the back of Eisner's Ultramar, its body shivering in the cold rain. He was that cat now, wet and dry, hot and cold, caught in the open without a wall to plaster himself against. The urge to run swept up and over him but he forced himself to stand still, his mind already blocks away in the darkness. "I just wanted you to know," he finished quietly.

She'd said nothing for a moment, only looked at the ground, then at the paper in her hands. Suddenly humiliated and angry at himself for breaking his own rule, for becoming visible, Ben stepped backwards off the walkway onto damp grass, wanting only to melt into the shadows before anyone else came through that library door. He was just turning when he heard, "Ben?"

He stopped. Looked back.

"Do you have a last name?"

It was his turn to say nothing for a moment. Then, almost inaudibly, "Corbett."

She smiled a broad, radiant smile that made the streetlight above their heads seem candle-like and far away. "Thank you, Ben Corbett."

They walked and talked for nearly two hours that evening, and Ben was amazed at the ease with which Ann shared her life. She and her mother had just moved there from Bridgewater following her parents' divorce. "A place to start over," her mother had told her. Ann said it had more to do with her grandparents' moving to Florida than anything the town offered — her Gram and Grandad owned a condominium on Riverside Drive they didn't want to sell, and Ann's mother had spent enough money in her lifetime to recognize the sensibleness of rent-free living. Her divorce settlement had been substantial, but shopping was like breathing for her and what she didn't spend on rent or a mortgage was that much more she could spend on herself. And Ann, of course.

Ann had visited her grandparents many times in Brookdale, but she'd resented having to leave her friends and move there for good. Brookdale was a far cry from the bustle of Bridgewater. Even more disheartening was the fact that she could tell the people in the condominiums on either side of them weren't exactly thrilled about a family under fifty moving in. She'd seen it in their eyes and the way their veined hands gripped their canes and walkers as they stood watching her carry her stereo in from the moving van. She'd said hi but they'd nodded stiffly, absently, as if wondering whether the owner's agreement had a "No Teens" as well as a "No Pets" clause.

She'd gone to the library that night because she'd been tired of unpacking boxes and arguing with her mother. She'd also gone because she had belonged to a writers' group at her old school and because she thought it might be a good place to meet people her own age. She'd almost laughed out loud when she'd seen the people who were there — four of them she recognized from Riverside Drive.

She'd left the library prepared to deliver an ultimatum to her mother about moving back to Bridgewater. Then she'd met Ben. And discovered they'd probably be in some of the same classes when she registered at school the following day.

The library had been their beginning.

And now Ben held her on those same library steps, frightened that if he let go she'd be gone forever.

6

They walked without talking, avoiding Commercial Street and Merchant Avenue where Friday night shoppers and bored high school kids filled the brightly lit sidewalks, choosing instead to roam the quiet residential side streets that stretched all the way to the river. They stayed south of Main, a universe away from the little bungalow across from Freemont's Lumber Yard.

Finally Ann spoke. "Are you sure you can't go? Maybe if you explained to him how important it is." But it sounded ludicrous even to her. She had never met Rankin, knew him only from the things Ben had told her — and from the marks on Ben's face she'd seen when she'd stopped by his house that first time, the only time.

****

Except for those classes they didn't share, they'd been together constantly at school, including every recess and noon hour and the fifteen minutes between last bell and the time Ben had to be home. They'd talked endlessly about books and writers, about global warming and the trouble in the Middle East, about madness and movies and mysticism and music. And, finally, about love. Then in November when Ben suddenly was absent from school for two days, she'd been worried. He'd told her never to phone him, that his stepfather worked shifts and if he was sleeping the phone would disturb him. Ben had also told her never to go to his house, but by the second day she was worried and she'd headed there right after school.

Walking down North Street, she'd hoped Ben's stepfather was at work. Ben had said little to her about his family, but the look in his eyes whenever Rankin's name came up had made her uneasy. Now she wished she'd asked him more, pressed him further for answers. When she came to the little house across from the mill, she'd felt wary, unsure of herself, and she'd stood at the end of the gravel driveway for nearly a minute before mustering the courage to go on.

It wasn't that the house before her contrasted so sharply with the luxurious condominiums on Riverside Drive. Unlike both her parents, Ann cared little about where people lived, the cars they drove, the clothes they wore, one of the qualities that Ben most admired in her but that her own mother and father found mystifying. Her father, who owned an electronics store in Bridgewater, never failed to tell her — on those rare occasions they spoke — that appearances were everything. It was he who'd insisted on the braces. "You never get a second chance to make a first impression," he was fond of saying, and it was about the only thing her mother agreed with him on. Herself the consummate consumer, she could never understand why her daughter didn't share her enthusiasm for clothes and shopping in general. And Ann had given up trying to explain it. Clothes, as far as Ann was concerned, were purely functional. They should keep you warm or cool and, above all, they should be comfortable. Perhaps it was because for years Ann had watched her mother fret over which outfit to wear, had watched her wobble on impossibly high heels or clop about in unforgiving flats, had watched her sit stiffly so that every fold and crease was as it should be. She reminded Ann of those limited edition china dolls that were always being advertised in *McCall's* and *Ladies' Home Journal*, miniature women with names like "Felicity" and "Victoria" forever frozen in elegant poses. There were times when she'd have given anything to come home from school to find her mother lounging about in bathrobe, hair curlers, and fuzzy slippers.

No, it wasn't the appearance or even the location of Ben's house that made her feel uneasy. It was something else, something she couldn't put a finger on. She'd had feelings about things before that she couldn't ignore. Like the night last winter when she'd been unable to get to sleep. She had rolled about in her bed more than an hour before a call from Ontario had come. Her sister Meredith in her first year at the University of Toronto had mistakenly eaten a seafood hors d'oeuvre that had triggered an allergic reaction. The doctor who had telephoned assured Ann's mother that Meredith was out of danger but Ann hadn't slept at all that night, afraid that feeling might return. Standing across from Ben's house, she'd felt as though it had.

She'd knocked on the door three times before it finally opened a crack. A woman with dark hair pulled back into a bun peered through the opening and told Ann that, whatever she was selling, she had no use for it.

"I'm not selling anything," Ann had said quickly as the woman's face disappeared and the door began to close. "I go to Ben's school. I was just wondering if he was all right."

The face reappeared. "You're a friend of Ben's?"

Ann resisted the temptation to say they were more than friends. Ben was the first person she thought about when she woke up and the last person on her mind when she went to sleep. She had never dreamed she could feel so close, so connected, to another human being in the few weeks she had known him. It was as if he was a part of herself that she'd never even known was missing. But she'd replied simply, "Yes."

The door had opened further, enough to reveal half of the woman and a partial view of the kitchen behind her. Ann noticed there was nothing on the walls. Not even a calendar. There were, however, marks that looked like indentations in the plaster. "Ben's in bed," said the woman. "He has the flu."

"I thought he must be sick," Ann said. "Is there anything he needs? Anything I can get for him?"

The woman looked at her closely and Ann had the odd feeling that something had passed between them, but she didn't know what. "No, but thanks. He'll be fine in a day or two. It's one of those things that has to run its course."

"Would he like me to bring him his homework? I can get it from his teachers if he wants it." She felt stupid offering to bring him work while he was sick, but she wanted to do something, anything.

"Thanks, but Ben's good at catching up. He can get it when he goes back. I'll tell him you were here, though. He'll be pleased." The door started to close again.

"My name's Ann," she'd said just before it shut, then found herself looking at cracked and peeling paint that had long ago given up any pretence of colour.

She'd felt surprised and confused and embarrassed, wanted to see Ben yet, at the same time, wanted to be as far from North Street as she could get. She'd hurried down the steps and across the dead November weeds that masqueraded as a lawn in summer, not even bothering to use the driveway. Just as she'd come around the corner of the house she'd glanced back. There in a tiny window above her was Ben's face. She'd opened her mouth, but not in a greeting. Without knowing it, she'd uttered a thin cry and the face was gone.

* * * *

She looked up at Ben's face now, half expecting to see the dark bruise that had framed the left side of the face she'd seen in the window that day. Without thinking she reached up to touch his cheek and, even now, after all this time, he pulled back. She wondered if there would ever come a time when he would not flinch when she touched him.

"Talking to him about it is the last thing I could do," Ben said quietly. "He'd never let me go. Not after the last time he let me go someplace."

Ann knew about the outing with the Rockport Teens for Christ. She knew about everything. She'd made him tell her when she'd finally seen him three days after her visit to his house. He had brushed by her in the hall at recess mumbling something about having to arrange to write a makeup test for Mrs. Wentworth. At noon Ann couldn't find him anywhere, and she'd nearly given up waiting for him after school. Finally, though, he had come out of the building and she could tell he was surprised to see her still there. He'd kept his face turned away, but looking closely she could see the yellow shadow of the bruise beneath his skin.

It had taken a while, but she had let him tell it his way. There had been many silences, long moments when she'd had to clench her teeth to keep from speaking, grinding her molars together precisely the way her orthodontist, Dr. Shroeder, had warned her not to. But the words had eventually come, first individually, then in a trickle, then finally in a steady stream that at times she'd wanted to stop, wanted to plug her ears against and bury beneath a voice that cried silently, *No!*

And, afterwards, he'd sworn her to secrecy despite her assurances that there were people who could help, that what Rankin did was wrong and couldn't be allowed to continue. There was, he'd said, nothing anybody could do. He and his mother just had to try harder. And they did. Most of the time, it worked. Ben's absences from school told Ann when it didn't, and then she'd wait lifetimes by the phone willing it to ring, praying for it not to have been as bad as she imagined.

In her heart Ann felt Ben was wrong, but she couldn't take the chance of his being right. "I can't risk losing you," Ben had said as he'd clung to her, pleading for her promise of silence. And because she, too, could not risk losing him, she had given it freely.

Looking at him now, though, she could tell he was thinking of Mr. Lewis's letter, and she wondered if they could continue to pay the price of that silence. "Ben," she said quietly, "he's already made the last seven years hell for you. You can't do anything about that."

When she paused, he turned to her. "What makes me think there's a second part to what you're saying?" he asked.

"What about the rest of your life? You can't let him ruin that, too."

He suddenly stopped and looked at her closely. "What do you mean?"

"Lewis is right. This Summer Institute is the chance of a lifetime."

"Don't you think I know that?" Even in the weak light that filtered from the houses around them she saw a distance in his eyes, as if he was looking beyond her at something moving rapidly away in the darkness.

"You know it," she agreed. "But you haven't let yourself *feel* it. If you had, you'd do something about it."

His reply was almost a snarl, catching her off-guard. "What? What can I do about it? Tell me."

She reached for his hand and held it in both of hers, feeling the strength and helplessness like twins in his fingers. "You know what you can do, Ben. Maybe now is the time."

He looked away from her and didn't say anything for a while. When he did, it was as if he was speaking to someone else. "I've wanted to from the beginning," he said.

She said nothing, just squeezed his hand.

He turned to her again. "But you don't know him, what he can do." He tightened his fingers around hers. "You don't know what it's like to wake up in one place and go to sleep in another. To start everything all over again, not knowing if it's for a week or a month or a year, just knowing you'll never see any part of that other place again."

"But if you tell someone —"

"Who would believe me? He can be a completely different person when people are around. It'd be my word against his."

"What about —" But she stopped, reluctant to finish her thought.

She didn't have to. "My mother? She can't even *imagine* life without him. She's convinced we'd end up on the street."

"There are people who wouldn't let that happen."

"Her faith is in God. Not other people. She thinks she has a life here and prayer will make it perfect." Bitterness hardened his last comment and he shook his head in disgust.

"You have a life here, too," she reminded him.

He reached out and folded his arms around her. "And I'm not going to do anything that might ruin it."

Holding each other in the darkness they seemed like one person, two halves of a single body surrounded by night.

"So I guess that's that," she murmured finally into his shoulder.

"Yeah. That's that," he replied, his voice little more than a whisper.

7

Off in the distance, the yellow sky met the white ground in an unbroken straight line. There was no sound, no wind, no movement of any kind. It was like standing alone in the middle of a snow-covered prairie, except the snow was firm and flat and warm. It supported his weight as he stood there turning his head from left to right, scanning the horizon for something he could not see yet knew was there. And, before long, it was.

The edges of the horizon rippled, undulated, and the once flat landscape now pulsed with shapeless forms that rose out of the whiteness around him. Themselves white, they cast no shadows, and he was unsure of how he could see them against the ivory terrain. And then he knew he wasn't seeing them. Instead, he *felt* their presence in front of him, behind him, all around him, at first remote, then closer, like the walls he could always sense when he stood near them with his eyes shut. Yet he was unafraid.

Then the whispering began, distant voices like sleet against glass, incessant and wordless yet full of purpose and meaning. He strained to distinguish sounds, syllables, a semblance of language, then realized — as he had realized so many times before — that the voices whispered names. Then, of course, he knew it was only one name, his name, repeated over and over, again and again so that each utterance blended with the one before and after it, a slow chant that rose higher and higher until it, too, took on form and function like the turgid looming figures around him. And still he was not afraid.

The first touch was casual, almost accidental, the sensation like thick, warm fog against his skin. He stepped back in surprise, only to find himself pressing against more of that thick warmth, except beneath it he could feel something substantial, almost solid, pressing back. It was then that he remembered to be afraid.

The chanting had risen in pitch and volume, becoming jarring and cacophonous, fingernails on a white chalkboard that stretched down and down and down. He felt suddenly as if he were inside it or it inside him, as if a connection had been formed, umbilical-like, between himself and the sound, and one now sought to be borne of the other. He twisted his body forward and his elbow brushed across bulk — soft, white, meat-like resistance that rippled and then surged against him, pressing him, pushing him back.

He brought up his other arm but by now, of course, it was too late. There was only a white wall around him, pushing against him, crowding in on him, moving up and over him like a solid ivory tide. When he finally opened his mouth to scream, the white flowed into it forcing its way like a fist down his throat and out his nose. He couldn't even close his eyes.

* * * *

Ben woke with a scream clotted in his throat, his whole body drenched and shaking as he lay frozen on his mattress. He could feel beads of sweat slide down the sides of his upturned face, moving slowly at first, then gaining speed as they joined other droplets, finally soaking into the worn sheet beneath him. His hands shook as they gripped the single blanket that covered him, and he forced his fingers to relax their hold — one at a time — on the old flannel. By breathing in and out carefully through his mouth he could ease the frantic gasping he'd woken to, and soon even the hammering in his chest had slowed to a uniform beat. He lay there a few more minutes, then sat up and slid his legs over the edge of the mattress. Since the mattress lay on the linoleum, his legs were nearly parallel to the floor as he sat motionless, listening to the night sounds around him. From the room across the hall came Rankin's grunt-like snores, each beginning with a sudden suction and ending with a long, bibbering murmur. Ben could never hear his mother in the dark. He once thought it was because Rankin's night noises were so loud they drowned out any she made, but then he'd discovered she rarely slept. Once when he was about nine — he remembered they were living in Jake's Bay because he was sleeping on an old cot in the front room — he'd gotten up in the middle of the night to pee. Padding softly past his mother and Rankin's open bedroom door, he'd looked in. The window was curtainless and moonlight fell in a broad slash across the bed. Beside the huge, snoring bulk that was his stepfather lay his mother, her eyes wide and staring at the ceiling overhead, her hands folded above the blankets. Her lips moved silently and Ben had stood there for a minute or more watching, wondering even then if anyone, anything, could be listening to those silent words. Then she'd turned towards him and he'd seen something pearl-like glistening in the corner of one eye. He'd turned around and slipped quietly back to his cot. From then on, he'd made sure he went to the bathroom before going to bed.

One street over a dog barked, and then from the opposite direction came the answering howl of a hound. Many of the houses along North and Station Streets had at least one dog and, if a raccoon or skunk happened by, they could create a din that would surge back and forth along the three blocks west of the mill, sometimes echoing as far away as Empire Heights. The two times it had happened that spring, the police had received half a dozen complaints and had issued warnings immediately to the dogs' owners. Apparently, dogs in the Heights barked only when necessary, and never after nine o'clock at night.

Ben crossed his fingers that a raccoon hadn't gotten into the garbage. He had no fondness for those masked thieves, but nothing deserved Rankin's wrath for having wakened him in the middle of the night. Luckily, there was no answering bark from the first dog and everything was quiet again.

Ben reached for his watch in the darkness, found it on top of the milk crate, and squinted to make out the positions of the hands beneath the cracked crystal. There would be no more sleep that night — he'd had the dream enough times to learn that — and he wanted to know how long he would have to wait this time before it was safe to get up. Twenty minutes after four. Nearly two hours yet. He cursed silently, then lay back against the mattress. His back immediately found the damp spot his sweat had made and he rolled carefully over to the other side.

Gazing up at the ceiling, he tried to remember all the other ceilings he'd slept under in his lifetime. Before Rockport and Jake's Bay there had been Hackett's Cove and Martin's River, and before that Edgartown on the foggy South Shore.

Brookdale was the farthest inland they'd ever lived, and Ben still missed the mournful hoot of foghorns and the clang of channel markers rocking on the swell. What he missed most, though, was the time before Rankin, the time when only Ben and his mother slept under their ceilings.

Ben's father had walked — no, run — out on them just before Ben's sixth birthday. Ben didn't remember much about his father, just that he was quiet and hardly spoke — unless he was drinking. Those times he could afford a bottle, he would have plenty to say. Ben could remember few of the words but he recalled like yesterday how they made his mother cry.

Ben's parents had married young — he was seventeen and she was sixteen — and Ben didn't need to be told he had been the reason for the wedding. Both had dropped out of school before Ben was born, and his father had worked in the woods while his mother had stayed home to care for the baby. She took in washing and mending to help make ends meet, but a lot of times those ends didn't even come close.

Ben never knew his grandparents. His father had been raised in an orphanage in Dartmouth until he was four, then had been shunted about from foster home to foster home in the years that followed. And once his mother's parents had given legal permission for the marriage, they would have nothing more to do with her; they'd repeatedly warned their only child to stay away from the boy they'd said was interested in only one thing, and now that she'd made her bed she'd damn well better lie in it. They'd died in a house fire before Ben's first birthday, and what little they'd left behind had gone to pay funeral expenses. They had never seen their grandson.

Ben's mother and father lived first in a trailer park near Fox Cove, then in a run-down tenement in Shank's Harbour. Ben remembered little about those early years other than the fact that he was often hungry and there had been plastic covering many of the windows of the places they lived in. The rest was a blur of bad times and worse. Finally, a day came when his father didn't come home, followed by a week of waiting. Each day as Ben watched his mother make meals out of nothing — tomato soup from ketchup and water, chicken broth from a bouillon cube — he'd see her eyes stray to the window that overlooked the highway, searching for the red toque she'd knitted for her husband the Christmas before. It never appeared. In its place came a paper the landlord wedged in the kitchen window when his mother wouldn't answer the door. She'd left it there all that afternoon like a small white flag flapping in the wind; it wasn't until darkness had fallen that she finally brought it in. There'd been no supper that night and Ben's stomach had growled and groaned as she'd held him and the letter far into the evening, whispering softly to him words he didn't understand. Then, abruptly, she'd put him down and rooted through some drawers until she found a pencil. Tearing the landlord's paper into several strips, she wrote something on each of them in her small, careful lettering, then folded them into tiny squares and laid them on the plywood table. Hugging Ben to her, she'd told him to pick one. He did and she'd unfolded it slowly, looking at it a long time before finally putting Ben to bed. The next day she'd packed everything they owned into a cardboard box and a battered green suitcase and they'd stood on the highway with their thumbs out.

They'd hitchhiked to Edgartown, getting a ride from a trucker who opened a can of sliced pears with a jackknife and gave it to them. It was the first time Ben had ever eaten canned pears, and on his empty stomach their sweet syrup had seemed like five kinds of ice cream. The trucker talked constantly about the road and his rig, about the people he'd met and the places he'd been, the blurp and buzz of his CB punctuating his endless stream of words. Then he had asked Ben's mother what was waiting for them in Edgartown.

"I don't know yet," she'd said, her eyes focused on some faraway point beyond her window.

The pavement had whined by under the eighteen wheels and no one said anything for a while. Then the trucker had started talking again, this time about a friend named Ray Leonard and his wife, Joanne, who owned a small business on the western end of town. "R & J's Used Books it's called," the trucker had said. "There's a small apartment over top of the store that I think is still empty. Wouldn't cost you much. I could take you right there. I don't have to be at my drop-off till three."

He had been right. The apartment above R & J's Used Books was still empty and the Leonards — a sympathetic couple in their early forties who had moved to Nova Scotia from Philadelphia — were willing to forgo the first month's rent until their new tenant got a job. It wasn't much of an apartment anyway, they'd apologized, and they'd been right. A single large room, it was an add-on that had served as a storage area for all four of the businesses that had operated beneath it in the previous thirty years. The Leonards had tucked a bathroom behind the stairwell and added a fridge, stove, table, and bed bought fourth-hand at an auction, but it still wasn't much more than a box with windows, an opinion shared by the previous tenant who had stayed only eight days.

To Ben and his mother, however, it was everything they needed. The rent was reasonable. There was a diner nearby that was always hiring waitresses, and she had gotten a job there the next day. The town's elementary school was just up over the hill and Ben could easily walk there and back by himself when his mother was working. But the best part was the books in the store below.

Ben's first year in Edgartown revolved almost entirely around the building that contained R & J's Used Books. Although he enjoyed school, he would race out as soon as the last bell rang, hurrying past kids playing marbles or bouncing balls despite their invitations to join them. He'd run all the way to the diner or up the stairs to the tiny apartment, stopping only when he was certain his mother was still there. She always was. But he always had to make sure.

Sometimes when his mother was working at the diner, Ben would drift into R & J's and wander about the shop that smelled alternately of salt air or must, depending on whether the windows were open or closed. Neither Joanne Leonard nor her husband minded his being there; he was quiet and well mannered and, they discovered, a big help when it came to sorting paperbacks and putting them on the countless shelves Ray had built out of spruce boards and plywood.

In the beginning, the reason for the different sections eluded him: why worry about where one book went and another didn't? But Joanne Leonard had answered that question and all the others he asked in the months that followed. Having had her tubes tied after two miscarriages, she was childless, and she liked having this child around, enjoyed sharing with him what she knew about books — which was considerable since her mother had been a librarian for fourteen years. And he learned quickly. Before long he could tell by its cover whether a book belonged in the section marked Mystery or Romance, Horror or Adventure, Western or Science Fiction, or on the shelves marked Non-fiction or Adolescent at the back of the store. Soon he wasn't just looking at the cover

— he discovered the magic of black marks on paper, marks that held meaning, painted pictures, made movies inside his mind. By the following year he was reading everything Joanne would lend him.

He'd started first with children's books, but he'd soon found them predictable, knowing by the middle of the first chapter how they would end. So Joanne had introduced him to Robert Louis Stevenson, Sir Arthur Conan Doyle, J. R. R. Tolkien, writers who showed him that there were worlds beyond even his own imagining that could be reached through the written word. Often his mother would arrive home to find him sitting at the table in their apartment, so absorbed in *Kidnapped* or *The Hound of the Baskervilles* that she'd had to touch his shoulder to let him know she was there. Eventually she'd found him sitting just as absorbed with a pencil in his hand, scribbling furiously on scrap paper and brown grocery bags, creating worlds peopled by characters of his own making. Although she was often tired beyond belief, she'd sit beside him while he read aloud what he'd written, his face shining with excitement.

Those were the best times. They had little to call their own but they had a roof over their heads, money to buy food and pay the rent, and good friends in the Leonards. At Joanne's invitation, his mother had joined the Baptist Church on Dock Street and attended every Sunday she wasn't working, taking Ben with her. She started reading the Bible every night, sharing with Ben stories from the Old and New Testaments, returning often to the one about Ruth who had gone through so much, yet survived. On several occasions, Ben's mother said God had delivered them to Ray and Joanne Leonard.

Ben no longer believed that. If God *had* done that, He had also allowed Ray to die of cancer their third winter in Edgartown, had allowed R & J's Used Books to go out of business when South Shore Video Rentals opened, and had allowed a group of Halifax businessmen to buy the building — their home! — and tear it down to build a Tim Horton's. Even worse, God had allowed Jim Rankin to enter their lives.

Rankin had come into the diner around the time Joanne decided to sell. With Ray so sick she'd often had to close the store, at first so she could drive him to his radiation treatments in Halifax and then, later, just to be with him. At the end, when she again had time to worry about the business, South Shore Video had opened three doors down and it suddenly seemed like people didn't read books anymore. Even the housewives who once brought in their Harlequins and Silhouettes by the carton-full to exchange for newer romances now rarely came into R & J's. Four months after she'd buried Ray, Joanne put the For Sale sign on the building.

Rankin had been in the diner three times before, always sitting at the long counter Ben's mother worked behind rather than at one of the tables along the windows overlooking the harbour.

He'd chatted with her about working on the lobster boats that were tied up for the season, about the weather that made everything and everyone feel grey and moldy, about the lack of anything for a single man to do in Edgartown, and, eventually, about the lack of a ring on the third finger of her left hand.

With the exception of polite conversation with regular customers and occasional banter with Mac Ingersoll, the owner and cook, Ben's mother had talked rarely to anyone besides Joanne and Ray. She began to look forward to this big stranger who always sat on the same stool and ordered the same thing from the menu: hamburg steak with gravy. Then, the afternoon Joanne told her she was selling the building, Ben's mother had gone to work with red eyes. The stranger — who, by now, had a name — had asked her about those red eyes, had reached across the counter, putting his big hand over hers, and had told her if there was anything at all that he could do . . .

The first night she'd brought him home to meet Ben, he'd laughed a lot, a big booming laugh that made Ben feel uneasy even then, as if it had strength and a will of its own echoing about the little apartment, reaching into every corner, filling the place with its presence, and making Ben feel even smaller than he was. Ben was glad when the man and his laugh had gone but, looking at his mother as she waved from the street-side window, he knew something had changed for them. And it would never be the same again.

When Joanne came to them with the news that the building had sold, Rankin was there. He was there again when the notice of eviction arrived from Halifax telling Ben's mother they had three months to vacate the building before demolition began. Ben's mother had sobbed when she'd read it and Rankin had folded her in his thick arms and held her, told her not to worry, he'd take care of her, all the while looking over her shoulder at Ben, his eyes dark and unmoving.

The wedding had happened faster than Ben thought possible. He had not known his mother had signed divorce papers two years earlier at Ray and Joanne's urging. He had not known his mother would ignore his feelings, his warnings about Rankin. He had not known how little was involved in the ceremony of marriage.

And neither of them had known Rankin would make them leave Edgartown before the ink was dry on the marriage certificate.

Gazing up into the darkness, Ben could see the first fingers of morning reach across the ceiling, disproving once again the lie about it being darkest before the dawn. Ben knew exactly when the darkest times came, and they had nothing to do with the light of day.

8

"Anybody home?" Ben called as he opened Sadie's porch door. He always knocked twice before entering, but he'd learned long ago that Sadie seldom heard knuckles rapping unless she had her hearing aid turned on — which wasn't often since batteries were "so dear," as she described them. At the end of a month there wasn't a lot left over from her widow's allowance and old age pension for "extravagances." Ben had often marvelled at this assessment of her hearing as being somehow superfluous, relegated to the status of a commodity she could do without, but then again she was a woman who had learned to do without all her life.

"Hello?" he called again, louder. "Are you home, Sadie?"

"Come in if you're out," came a voice. It sounded like water flowing over gravel, low and thick but layered with music. Ben often paused outside her house on the way to and from school just to listen to that voice. When the weather was warm Sadie's windows would be up, and through them he could hear her sing "Rock of Ages," "Bringing in the Sheaves," "He's Got the Whole World in His Hands," and other old hymns that floated out on the air and above the whine of the saws in Freemont's mill. It was the holiest sound Ben had ever heard, holier even than "Silent Night" chiming on the church carillon on Christmas Eve. If he believed in a god, that god would have a voice like Sadie's.

She was sitting in her rocker by the kitchen table, her Bible spread open on her lap, and her thin wrinkled face split into a wide grin when she saw him. "Ben," she said, reaching up and touching a button on the back of her hearing aid, "I was hoping you'd be over this morning."

"Hi, Sadie. Mom asked me to pick up those banana breads you two made last night. They smell good," he said, nodding towards the five fat loaves that lay on racks on the counter by the stove.

She waved away his compliment. "Your mother's doing," she said. "She wouldn't even let me pour out the flour." She shook her head. "After standing all day on her feet, she spent over an hour last night mashing and mixing, so that's why I told her I'd mind the oven and then shooed her home."

She smiled again. "I'm glad she sent you to fetch them, though. There's something I wanted you to hear. Sit down." Ben glanced at his watch: 9:25. The loaves didn't have to be at the church until ten o'clock so he pulled a chair out from the table and sat down. He always had time for Sadie.

He remembered the first time he'd come there, returning the dish she'd brought over filled with apple crisp that first day. He'd been homesick for Rockport — even for that dingy apartment in back of Eisner's Ultramar — and she seemed to sense it, inviting him in for diet Coke and introducing him to Leona, her blue budgie, and a cat named Elijah that Sadie said lived with her but belonged to no one. That was the first of many such visits, and it wasn't long before Ben knew he'd find her doing one of two things: reading the Bible or writing. At first he thought she was making up grocery lists because she never filled the lines, her words like ladders on the page. She always put them away when he arrived but once she'd dropped one on the floor and, bending to retrieve it for her, he'd noticed her grocery list had a title.

That was the day he learned Sadie was a poet. Of course, she didn't call herself that. "A note-jotter" was the way she described herself. "I see things that remind me of other things and I jot them down." Ben had smiled. That was probably the best definition of a writer he'd ever heard. Soon after that he'd shared with Sadie one of the stories he had written, and they'd been each other's biggest fans ever since.

"Care for something to eat?" she asked.

"No thanks. I just finished breakfast." That, of course, was a lie. He'd been up as soon as Rankin had stirred across the hall, and he'd boiled oatmeal on the hot plate — his stepfather only ever ate cooked meals — and cleaned up the dishes even before his mother had left for Save-Easy and Rankin had walked to Cruikshank's. But somehow it was important to have Sadie believe he slept in on Saturday mornings. Most teenagers his age did. At least, that's what he'd heard.

"Sure? I baked bread yesterday. Maybe just a slice?"

Ben thought of Pavlov's dogs and smiled. The scientist had conditioned the animals to salivate at the sound of a bell. Sadie could make his mouth water by just mentioning her bread. "Okay. Just one. Want me to get it?"

"You just stay put. I can still wait on a gentleman caller," she quipped, then set her Bible on the table and eased herself out of her rocker. Ben watched as she moved slowly about the kitchen, noticed how gingerly she slid her feet over the tile floor. Her arthritis was always at its worst in the morning and he remembered how she'd described it in one of her poems:

> a red snake coiled round my brittle bones,
> tongue forking fire as it squeezes
> the breath from my lungs.

Amazingly, though, she thanked God for that snake. "Makes me appreciate every day I get out of that bed," she'd told him. "A lot of old women just lie under their sheets and watch the day go by. I have my snake to wrestle with each morning, and after I put him in his place I'm ready for most anything." She went to the cupboard and opened up a tin breadbox her husband had made for her long before Ben's mother was born. She took out a double loaf of white bread, its top crust nearly the same colour as her hands. "Only one?" she asked.

"Just one," he replied.

"I'll cut a couple just in case," she said.

He smiled. How well she knew him.

She pulled a long steel knife out of a drawer, its blade narrow and crescent-shaped from years of sharpening. She gripped its handle in her left hand, held the loaf against the countertop with her right, and sawed the knife back and forth. Ben watched those dark hands, gnarled and ugly yet strangely beautiful, as they cut one thumb-thick slice, then another.

Ben was fascinated by Sadie's hands and had watched them many times as she'd worked in her flowerpots, turned the pages of her Bible, held glasses of diet Coke, smoothed her crinkled white hair behind her ears, waved in the air while she sang. But it was when she made bread that Ben most liked to watch them, mesmerized by the way they moved, the way they looked against the flour like black birds flying over snow. They looked more like the hands of a man than a woman. They would mold and knead the dough on the cracked oilcloth that covered the kitchen table as if trying to pull from it a message only they could read. She would push her swollen knuckles into it and then flatten it with the palms of her hands, finally shaping it into double loaves that Ben's imagination always saw as full, white breasts. Then she'd slide them into the oven for an indeterminate time. They would be done when she said they were done, not before or after, and no clock marked their progress. Sadie had little and cooked with less. "Making do," she called it. From scratch. But her bread was a living thing that spoke of miracles.

And it spoke volumes in Ben's mouth now as he chewed its white goodness slowly, savouring each morsel. Sadie's bread was a meal in itself and Ben liked eating it with nothing on it, not even butter, although Sadie always offered him jams and marmalades or cinnamon and sugar or, if she'd budgeted extra carefully that month, frozen strawberries she would thaw under hot water.

When she offered him the second slice, he didn't even try to refuse it. She wouldn't have allowed him to anyway. "So," he said around another mouthful, "what's this you wanted me to hear?"

Sadie lowered herself slowly into her rocker again and pulled her Bible onto her lap. It was a massive book as thick as Ben's arm, a gift from Sadie's husband the day they were married. In nearly every margin of every page were words pencilled in Sadie's spidery handwriting, thoughts she'd had each time she'd read through it. Ben could not even begin to guess how many times she'd read that book. Fifty, maybe. Possibly sixty. Sadie loved reading her Bible. "Each time I open it," she'd told Ben, "I find something I missed before. Something I know I read but didn't really see. Know what I mean?"

Sadie fanned the pages of the Bible until she got close to the end, then began turning them one by one. "Here it is," she said. "Jude. He was writing about unbelievers." She looked up and grinned. "No, this isn't a sermon for Ben Corbett. It was the way he described them I wanted you to hear." She lowered her head, adjusting her glasses with a twisted finger. "'These men are those who are hidden reefs in your love-feasts when they feast with you without fear, caring for themselves; clouds without water, carried along by winds; autumn trees without fruit, doubly dead, up-rooted; wild waves of the sea, casting up their own shame like foam; wandering stars, for whom the black darkness has been reserved forever.'" She looked up. "Aren't those beautiful? The comparisons, I mean. Clouds without water, autumn trees doubly dead. I've read Jude more times than I can count, but that's the first time I noticed the way he piled up his pictures there."

Ben smiled. "You're right. They *are* beautiful. The one about the clouds would make a great title, wouldn't it?"

"I think so, too." She waggled a finger at him.

"Now don't you go and steal it on me," she grinned. "I've been playing with a poem and I think I'll use that."

Ben put his hands up in surrender. "You found it, Sadie. It's yours." He took another bite of the bread. "Of course," he said slowly, his eyes lowered, "if you don't publish your poems, who would know I got it from you?"

She cocked an eyebrow at him. "Ben, this isn't going to be another one of your push-Sadie-to-the-post-office routines, is it?"

Ben looked at her. "Sadie, your poems are terrific. I bet there are a lot of people who'd love to publish them. But you'll never know till you actually send them away."

She looked at him fondly. "Now *there's* the pot calling the kettle black. When was the last time you sent any of *your* stories away?"

He grinned sheepishly. "Okay, okay. But it's a shame no one gets to read them except me."

"No more a shame than no one seeing those stories you write." She reached her hand across the table and touched his. "Ben, I don't write my poems for anyone to read." She smiled. "Except you, of course. You're different. But I could no more show anyone else my poems than I could go to church wearing my bloomers for a hat. Land, boy, Lilly Mansfield and Rowena Porter would be on the phone to Willow Park before you could say shoot."

Ben chuckled. Willow Park was the mental hospital over in Kings County.

"I write my poems for myself and that's all. But you," she said, squeezing Ben's hand, "your stories are for everybody. You could *do* something with your stories. Maybe be a writer for real and earn your living writing. *You're* the one who needs to make the trip down to the post office."

Ben felt his face go warm and the bread in his mouth was suddenly tasteless. He laid what was left of the second slice on the table. "Sadie —" he began.

"Don't you Sadie me," she scolded softly. "You're young. You have your whole life in front of you. What do you plan to do with it?"

He didn't say anything for a long moment. Ann had asked him the same thing and he hadn't had an answer for her, either. Finally, "I'm like you. I write because I like to write. But there are only a handful of people in all of Canada who make their living doing just that and nothing else. Most do other things to pay the bills. They teach, sell real estate, cut hair, bathe dogs. I'll never be one of the handful. I'm not good enough."

"Maybe not now," she said, "but you're already better than most. Better than the ones who write those books I see in the drugstore, anyway, and they churn them out left, right, and centre. You can *learn* what you need to know. What about college?"

Ben could not mask the sarcasm in his voice. "I'm having too much trouble deciding between Queen's and Carlton. I just can't seem to make up my mind." When she didn't laugh, he softened.

"Look, Sadie, people like me don't go to college."

"What do you mean, people like you?"

"In case you haven't noticed, this isn't Empire Heights. And my mom doesn't own that mill out there."

Sadie looked across at him, her eyes wide behind her glasses. "Ben, lots of people work their way through college. Everybody doesn't have their way paid."

"Have you looked at tuition costs lately? I have. They're crazy. And I heard on the news that a lot of universities are putting them up another ten percent this fall. Someone like me doesn't have a chance."

Neither said anything for a minute. In the living room, Leona chirped and warbled and rattled around in her cage. A truck loaded with logs rumbled past the house and into Freemont's, its air brakes hissing as it lurched to a stop. Ben looked down at his watch and saw that it was 9:50. He pushed his chair back and stood up. "Thanks for the bite, Sadie, but I've got to get those banana breads over to the church."

Sadie got up slowly and took two plastic bags out of the closet by the fridge and put three of the loaves into one and two into the other.

"I thought one of those was for you," Ben said.

"Your mother wouldn't've let me give her the flour and sugar if I hadn't said I'd keep one. The church needs it more than me, though. What she doesn't know won't hurt her. Our secret?" she asked.

Ben nodded and reached for the bags.

Sadie didn't hand them over right away. "I know you're in a hurry, but there's something I want to tell you. It'll just take a minute."

Ben looked at her. He knew what he'd said had upset her, maybe even offended her somehow. There was something in her eyes that seemed suddenly sad. He didn't want to leave her like that. "All right."

Sadie passed him the bags, then moved over to her rocker again and sat down. Looking up, she asked, "Do you know the house on School Street across from the Legion?"

"Which one?"

"Little grey one with the carport."

"Yeah, I know the one you mean. What about it?"

"Riley Grangeford owns it. Do you know Riley?"

"He sings in your church choir, doesn't he?"

She raised her eyebrows. "I'm surprised you know that," she teased.

Ben smiled. "Last month Mom made some sandwiches for the Easter fellowship and she asked me to pick up the plate the next evening. The choir was rehearsing in the sanctuary and I listened for a minute. I asked Mom later who Riley was. He has a good voice," he added.

That, of course, hadn't been the reason he'd noticed Riley, and Sadie knew it. "Notice anything besides his voice?" she asked.

Ben smiled weakly. "You mean the fact that he's black?" Riley's seventy-year-old face had stood out among the white faces around him.

"Yes," said Sadie. "The fact that he's black."

"What about it?"

"Riley didn't always live on School Street."

"Where did he live?"

"On the other end of North. Down by the swamp."

"Okay. So what?"

Sadie leaned back in her chair and rocked slowly back and forth, once, twice. She seemed to be going over in her mind the words she wanted to say. Finally, "Riley and his wife worked hard all their lives and saved every cent they didn't spend on their four kids. Thirteen years ago, Riley and Althea had enough money to buy that house, and they did."

"So this is a story about saving money? Sadie, I'd need to save —"

"No," she interrupted, "this isn't a story about saving money. Do you know where the train used to run through town before they tore up the tracks?"

"Sure."

"Where is Riley's house compared to those tracks?"

"South of them. Why?"

"Thirteen years ago, there wasn't a black family in Brookdale that lived south of those tracks."

Ben thought for a moment. "So Riley was the first. What does that have to do with me?"

"One night thirteen years ago, Riley walked over to Harold and Ethel Bignall's house and then Bill Llewellyn's after that. They own the houses on either side of the grey one. At least, Bill used to. I don't know who lives there since he passed on. Anyway, they didn't know Riley and Riley didn't know them, except to nod his head to on the street. He went there that night to ask if they would mind him buying the house next door that just went up for sale." She paused to let that sink in, then repeated it. "He asked if they would mind."

Ben shook his head. "Wow," he said softly.

"Now, Brookdale's not like Halifax and Dartmouth. We don't have the things happen here that happen in those cities. But part of it was here just the same, is *still* here." She stopped, groping for a word. "A distance, I guess you'd call it. Under all the nods and smiles and how-do-you-do's. A distance. And not just the distance between North Street and the rest of town. You know what I mean."

"I know what you mean," Ben said, thinking of a lawn in front of a house in Empire Heights. He knew.

"What I'm trying to say here is that there aren't — how'd you say it? — 'people like you.' At least, there shouldn't be. Just like there shouldn't be 'people like me.' All of us are people. You got it in your head that you're different somehow than the people who can afford to go to college. And not just money-wise. Sure you're different in the things that make each of us different. But you're just as good. You shouldn't ever think you aren't. You don't ever have to ask for someone's permission to do or be whatever you want." She looked down at her dress, suddenly embarrassed. "I don't mean to preach. Reverend Richards does it better than me anyhow." She looked up at him again. "But you understand what I'm telling you, Ben?"

Ben looked at this wise old woman sitting in front of him. "Yes, Sadie, I understand." He crossed the kitchen and put his hand on her arm. "Thank you."

She reached up and patted his hand. "Now you get going or you'll be late with those banana breads."

Outside the sun was warm and so bright that Ben had to shield his eyes against it, but it did nothing to dispel the darkness in his heart, the feeling that he'd lied to his friend. Walking down North Street, he thought again of the reason he'd given Sadie for not planning on college. Any life beyond Brookdale was as inaccessible as Everest, but money was only part of the reason. Fear was the other part. Not for himself, though. For his mother. There were times when the two of them together barely survived his stepfather's rages. What would happen if she were left behind with Rankin, alone?

The two plastic bags swung back and forth as he walked, brushing lightly against the sides of his legs. Even with this burden, though, he felt like Jude's autumn tree without fruit, doubly dead.

9

Ben sat on the bleachers at the far end of the soccer field waiting for the bell. Ann had already gone into the school. Although they shared the same English, math, and physics classes, they were in different homerooms and Ben didn't want her to be late. His homeroom teacher, Mrs. Belding, didn't mind people coming in after the bell as long as they made it before she sent the attendance slip down to the office. Mr. Wheeler, Ann's homeroom teacher, was anal retentive when it came to tardiness. Ben suspected that, given his way, Wheeler would have late students executed at dawn.

The first day back after the Victoria Day long weekend was a perfect one, par for the course after a Sunday and Monday of continuous rain. The soccer field still had a mini-lake near the goalposts at the west end, but the sun on Ben's back told him it would be gone before noon. That spring had brought with it some of the best growing weather the Annapolis Valley's farmers could remember, and the soccer field was already a thick carpet of green that reminded Ben of the lawns he'd seen in Empire Heights.

He shuddered slightly in spite of the heat on his back. It was because of his Friday afternoon in the Heights that he was sitting there now. Shay Phillips was also in Mrs. Belding's homeroom, and Ben wanted to avoid running into him before classes started. Shay had always been civil, but cool — Sadie's talk about "distance" came to mind — and he remembered a morning last fall when he'd gone to school earlier than usual. Rankin had been in a foul mood the day before and he'd gotten up that morning raging at everything Ben and his mother did. Since his stepfather was working 3 to 11 that week and would be home for hours, Ben had invented an excuse about needing to see a teacher for extra help. He'd expected no one but janitors to be at the school so early and, heading up the walkway to the main entrance, he'd been surprised to see Shay sitting on the front step. Probably an early basketball practice, Ben had thought as he smiled self-consciously and said hi. Shay had nodded but said nothing: a monarch surveying his kingdom, acknowledging a peasant. Embarrassed, Ben had hurried inside.

He was even more embarrassed today, and he had no intention of giving Shay an opportunity to comment on what had happened on his front lawn. He was probably inside telling Eddie and Carl and the rest about it right now, but at least Ben wouldn't have to listen to it. If he kept his head low, maybe they'd forget all about it.

And maybe *The National Enquirer* would win the Pulitzer Prize for news reporting.

The warning bell shrilled and Ben looked across the field to see the last of the stragglers file into the school, some taking last hurried puffs on cigarettes (spring had made the smokers bolder and they'd inched farther onto the school grounds every day), others shoving parts of lunches into their faces even before morning classes had begun. Ben jumped down off the bleachers but didn't head immediately towards the school; looking at his watch, he gave himself another minute out on the field, which would leave him twenty-five seconds to get to the building and into room 217 with, hopefully, no more than five seconds before the bell for first class. He pictured the smirk on Shay's face and wondered if he could shave that down to two seconds.

He set his books on the bleachers and made sure the tail of his long-sleeved shirt was tucked in and his cuffs were buttoned. Already the temperature on the field was in the twenties and that, combined with the mugginess left by two days of rain, was sure to make the school all but unbearable by noon. Ben silently cursed his shirt, knowing that by third period he'd be swimming inside it. What he'd give to be able to wear shorts and a T-shirt, and he thought again of Shay dressed in his tennis whites on the front step of that two-storey brick and clapboard colonial.

A lump formed in his throat and for a moment he allowed a wave of self-pity to wash over him. What must it be like, he thought, to live in a place like that, a place of perfect lawns and perfect lives, where all the rules are different, where the greatest concerns are what to wear next, what to drive next, what to be next. Where a single phone call about a barking dog can create a flurry of activity in the town hall and police headquarters and the home of Brookdale's mayor.

Ben swallowed hard, looked again at his watch, then picked up his books and began to jog across the field. By the time he reached the parking lot, a dark patch had already appeared on the back of his shirt.

* * * *

He had waited for nothing. Shay wasn't there, much to everyone's surprise since today was the final practice before the district's track-and-field competition on Wednesday. A natural athlete, Shay was favoured to win all four of his events, the one hundred metre a guarantee since he'd already broken in practice the record he'd set at the provincial competition the year before. Ben took his seat just moments before the first-class bell, thankful for the empty chair.

The morning crawled by, everyone — including the teachers — either still affected by long-weekend lethargy or brain-muddied with the heat. History followed double chemistry — a lab that proved experiments performed after a holiday weekend gave unreliable results — and Ben didn't see Ann again until fourth period English. He had looked for her at recess, but Sarah Horner said she'd been called to the office and the break had ended before he'd found her.

Ben had been too embarrassed to meet Mr. Lewis's eyes when he'd come into his classroom, had gone directly to his seat, and had put a lot of effort into getting his books out while watching the hallway for Ann who arrived only moments before the teacher shut the door.

Even in that oppressive heat, Mr. Lewis reached down inside their stupor and gripped each one of them. "Have you heard?" he asked the class in an exaggerated stage whisper.

"Heard what?" most of them chorused, accustomed to the teacher's unorthodox ways of introducing his lessons.

Suddenly his voice changed and he spoke with the halting, passionless monotone of a robot in a low-budget sci-fi film. "Last night the planet earth was destroyed, leaving alive only the eleven hundred fourteen creatures contained within this vessel you call a school. At present, we are streaking towards a star cluster in the Delta 4 Quadrant and shall arrive in approximately thirty-one of your earth minutes. The beings contained within this six-sided cell have been designated lawmakers responsible for creating a system of rules that will enable all occupants of this vessel to coexist in perfect harmony on the planet Baxter."

At this, several of the students laughed. George Baxter was the vice-principal in charge of discipline.

The teacher didn't miss a beat. "Your rules must be easily understood and few in number, and they must be agreed upon by every being in this room." He thrust out his arm stiffly and bent it sharply at a ninety-degree angle, looking at his watch. "You now have thirty minutes. Begin."

The class was galvanized, every member pulling his or her chair next to someone else, throwing out ideas, asking questions, arguing, jotting things down, crossing things out, laughing. Ben knew where this was headed — he'd seen a copy of *Lord of the Flies* on Mr. Lewis's desk after school on Friday — but that didn't stop him from enjoying the challenge the teacher had given them. He glanced around and found it difficult to believe several of these students were the same ones who had sat nearly comatose through history class the period before. Ann had ended up in a small group three rows over, and she was vigorously arguing with Clayton Caldwell while Marty Vanasse put his hands over his ears and shook his head. Through it all, Mr. Lewis walked stiff-legged around the room answering questions in the same halting monotone, never a moment out of character.

By the time the thirty minutes were up, the class had polarized into two camps, one made up of twelve members including Ben and Ann and, surprisingly, Clayton Caldwell, all of whom had adopted a humanitarian stance towards anticipating and solving the problems of their new society. The larger camp characterized itself by presenting hard-line, militaristic policies towards governing the planet. George Baxter himself couldn't have been more unforgiving, mused Ben.

When the class had all but erupted into a shouting match, Mr. Lewis held up his hands and the noise dissolved. "It appears you are at an impasse," he observed quietly.

There were murmurs of assent.

"Good," he said. Reaching under his desk, he pulled out a carton of books and began walking about the room, placing in front of every student a copy of William Golding's novel. "Perhaps you'll find the solution to your dilemma in here." He went on to tell a little about *Lord of the Flies* and then reminded all of them to keep their response logs handy as they read it. "I'll be interested in your reactions to the first chapter tomorrow," he said, his last sentence punctuated by the noon bell.

The teacher was standing just behind Ben's seat as he got up to leave. "Ben," Mr. Lewis said, "if you have a minute, could you stay behind?"

Ben suddenly thought of the film *Groundhog Day* in which Bill Murray relived the same twenty-four hours over and over again. He glanced over at Ann and asked, "Meet you on the soccer field?"

She smiled at him but her smile seemed unnatural, like the ones painted on porcelain dolls. Don't worry, he mouthed.

He remained seated. When everyone else had gone, Mr. Lewis sat down in the seat beside him. "Ben," he said, "I know we had this conversation Friday and I don't want you to think I'm pressuring you."

Ben looked at him blandly.

The teacher smiled. "Okay, okay," he said, "I'm pressuring you. I haven't yet contacted William Bradshaw to tell him you're not attending the Summer Institute. I plan to do it today if you're still adamant about not going, but I'm hoping I can change your mind."

Ben flattened his hands on the top of his desk, spreading his fingers apart. Sweat beaded between each one, leaving tiny smear marks on the smooth white surface. "I appreciate your interest, Mr. Lewis, but you can't."

"Let me try."

More droplets of sweat trickled from Ben's armpits and rolled down his sides, melting into the fabric of his shirt where it tucked into his jeans. He hadn't minded the heat during the class but now it seemed oppressive, like a hammer made of wool. Sweat rolled down his forehead and collected in his eyebrows. One large drop stung his eyes before he could wipe it away. "Mr. Lewis, I already told you how important this summer job is to me. If I miss two weeks —"

"With all due respect, Ben, I don't think you

fully appreciate the significance of your selection as an Institute participant. You're one of only twenty students in the whole country chosen for this. That's twenty out of seven hundred applicants!"

"I read the letter," Ben said drily.

"You read the words, Ben. But have you taken the time to consider the opportunity they represent? Surely that means more than two weeks' wages." Visibly agitated, the teacher ran his hand through his hair. "Don't you understand this is a chance of a lifetime?"

That line again. Chance of a lifetime. *Lifetime.*

The dam burst before Ben even recognized it was cracking. It was as though he was standing outside himself watching his own lips move, yet unable to stop them. "Of course I understand! Surely you know me better than that! I'd give anything to go!" He almost choked. *What are you doing?* he screamed at himself. *Shut up! SHUT UP!*

The teacher's face brightened. "I knew it!" he said, slapping his hand on the desktop. "So what's all this about not going?"

"I —". The wool hammer thudded against his face and for a second the room swam in front of his eyes. *Be Alert!* "I can't. I just can't."

"Why not, Ben?"

A dull pounding pulsed through Ben's head, like a door left unlatched in the wind. Pound, pound. *Be Alert!* Pound. *BE ALERT!* "I can't." *POUND. POUND!* "My stepfather —" He sucked in his breath, trying to draw the words back inside his body.

"What about your stepfather?"

Oh no "Nothing, really." *Oh no oh* "It's just that he's" *no no no no* "pretty strict about things like that." He couldn't breathe.

"Surely he'd understand —"

"Oh, sure, he'd understand." *nonononono* "It's just . . ." It was all unravelling, like yarn pulled off the needles. *NONONONONONONO*

"What, Ben? It's just what? Is it the money? The cost of expenses? Is that it?"

A lifeline, tossed about in a pounding surf. Ben grabbed it. "Yes. It's the money. We could never afford it."

"There's no charge for the Institute itself, Ben. Your lodging and meals are paid for by the Canadian Writers' Council. The only cost to you besides spending money is transportation there and back."

"My parents could never afford that. They don't make much money." Ben's face was hot, but it had nothing to do with the temperature of the room. He was ashamed, and not just of his lie. He suddenly felt as though he were standing in front of Shay Phillips's father. "Get out of here!" the man had screamed. As if Ben didn't belong there. Didn't belong anywhere but North Street.

Mr. Lewis smiled. "Ben, the money isn't a problem. There are funds that can provide financial help for a student in need."

Ben noticed he hadn't said "needy student" and the person standing outside himself was grateful for that much, at least. He knew, though, that the other Ben, the one sweating inside his long-sleeved shirt, the one whose right leg had begun to dance uncontrollably under his desktop, had to leave soon. If he stayed much longer, he'd crack right down the centre and everything would slip out on the floor.

The teacher's face was shining. "There are school bursaries and sponsorships by local organizations. The teachers set aside a portion of their staff dues to pay for special awards at the end of the year, and this could very well be considered one of those. Or student council could organize a fund drive. Any one of those could —"

Ben jerked to his feet, sending his chair flying into the desk behind him. The clack of plastic against metal grounded him and gave him something to focus on while he tried to make the two Bens one again. "Mr. Lewis, I just can't. That's all there is to it. I just can't." And he was gone.

* * * *

Ann knew something was wrong as soon as she saw him. His face looked like chalk and his hand trembled when she took it in hers. "What happened?" she asked.

He'd found her sitting on the bleachers in the same spot he'd waited earlier that morning. The heat had intensified, a white point under a magnifying glass. At least it meant they were alone — everyone else had retreated to the shade or fled to air-conditioned stores across town. He looked out at the field. He'd been right: the lake at the west end was gone. How he wished he could disappear as easily. "I almost blew it," he said.

He sat down beside her and told her what had happened. The telling somehow made it real, as if those moments in the classroom had been an illusion, a fantasy, and only now did they become actual. "I can't believe what I almost told him," he whispered when he'd finished, his voice toneless and hollow like the recorded phone number you got when you called Directory Assistance. "I could feel my mouth making the words and I couldn't stop it." He shook his head. "For a second I didn't even *want* to stop it. He kept asking me if I understood and I wanted to shout at him that *he* was the one who didn't understand." He took a ragged breath, let it out slowly, forced himself to breathe again.

"Maybe you *should* have told him."

He stared at her in disbelief. "What?"

She looked down at her bare feet, her sandals like tan footprints on the bleachers beside her. "Maybe it's time *someone* told."

"You don't mean that."

She touched both big toes together reminding Ben of those children in the Oscar Meyer commercials. "Yes, I *do*," she said softly.

"Why are you saying this?"

She looked up. "You want to, Ben. You said yourself you wanted to."

"Yes, but —"

She didn't let him finish. "Look at yourself.

What it's doing to you. You're throwing away what's probably the best thing to ever happen to you. You're a bundle of nerves ready to explode. You look like death warmed over. How long do you expect to go on this way?"

Despite the heat, Ben felt suddenly cold. "I thought it was only your *mother* who cared about the way people looked."

She frowned. "That's not fair."

"Isn't it?"

"You know it isn't. I wouldn't care if you painted your ears green and shaved your eyebrows if that's what you *wanted* to do." She looked at her feet again, her toes making figure eights in the grass. "I just think —" She paused. Finally, "I think it's time you stopped doing the things you *don't* want to do." She raised her eyes to his. "You can't keep this up forever."

"I've done it half my life."

"And where's it got you?"

He turned away. The heat, his meeting with Mr. Lewis, now Ann. Suddenly he wanted to say something to hurt her. To stop her from saying these things he didn't want to hear. "And your life with the Queen of K Mart is so perfect?"

He heard her sudden intake of breath. "At least she doesn't beat me black-and-blue and then wonder why supper is late."

Ben whirled to face her. "And this is somehow *my* fault?"

"Why are you twisting everything I'm saying?"

"Why are you attacking me like this?"

"I'm not! I'm —" Her voice trailed off.

"You're what?" he demanded.

"I'm afraid that if you don't tell, *I* will!" The words came in a rush, like gravel spun from beneath a tire. She looked away.

"What are you saying, Ann?"

Nothing.

"Ann?"

Still nothing. He was suddenly frightened. "Ann, what is it?"

"I called the police."

She could as easily have struck him. "You *what?*"

Her voice was very small. "The RCMP. I called them this morning."

He made a sound that was neither a moan nor a yelp but somehow both. A wordless startled cry.

She turned quickly. "I didn't talk to anyone. I hung up as soon as they answered."

He ran a trembling hand over his forehead. "But why?"

"I was called to the office at recess. Mother phoned and they'd put her on hold. You know how she likes being kept waiting." She laid her hands on her thighs, palm upward, as if waiting to receive the answer to the problem their lives had become. "After she'd hung up, I had the receiver in my hand and all I could think about was you sitting out here by yourself this morning, waiting till the last minute to go inside." She took a breath, exhaled slowly. "I thought about how you're always waiting. For things to change. To get better. And here was this Ottawa thing that might make a difference but you couldn't take advantage of it. It's like your whole life is on hold. I suddenly got very angry." She looked down at her open hands, then made sudden fists of them. "I wanted to tell them everything."

"But you didn't," Ben said softly.

She looked into his eyes. "I still want to, Ben. I want *you* to."

"Ann —" he began, but she cut him off.

"Don't say it, Ben." Her voice was barely audible, layered with defeat. "I don't want to hear it right now."

They sat silent for a while. Then, "You were wrong about one thing," Ben offered.

Ann sighed. "What's that?"

"About the Institute being the best thing that's ever happened to me." He put his face next to hers. "You are."

For the first time since he'd come onto the soccer field, she smiled.

He hugged her to him and they sat that way for a long moment. Then, "C'mon," she said. "We only have a few minutes before the bell rings and I've got a serious tuna sandwich here." She unzipped a purple nylon pouch with the words FEED BAG printed on its side and took out a large sandwich wrapped in cellophane. "Here," she said. "Have some."

He shook his head, but she wouldn't be refused. "Either this thing goes or I go," she threatened.

Ben took a bite and returned it to her. He noticed that she ate none of it, but said nothing.

"I've got some orange juice in here, too," she said and pulled out a plastic container.

As she poured some of the juice into a cup, Ben asked, "What did your mother call about?"

She looked up. "You mean the Queen of K Mart?"

Ben grimaced. "Sorry about that."

"Forget it. I guess I had it coming." She handed him the cup and he took a drink, then returned it to her. "Anyway, I was supposed to see Dr. Shroeder next week for my three-month checkup, but he's going to be out of his office. Some convention or something. So he moved up my appointment to nine o'clock tomorrow morning. Mother is supposed to pick me up at school this afternoon and drive me in to the city. We're going to spend the night with my Aunt Phyllis."

"Isn't she —"

"Yes, the plaid lady. Even her wallpaper is plaid. But she's a lot of fun. You'd like her." The unspoken "if you ever got to meet her" hung in the air between them. Ann took a swallow of the orange juice while not far from them a robin landed, its head bobbing into the grass. As she always did when she saw birds, Ann wished she could fly. Wished they could both fly, their powerful wings pushing the air and Brookdale behind them.

"So," Ben said finally. "When will you be back?"

"My appointment is just routine stuff so we should be in and out. Depending on the traffic, we could be back by noon. That is, if I can keep Mother out of the malls."

"I'll miss you," Ben said softly.

"You'd better," she warned. She smiled again, but her cheeks were doing all the work. Her eyes, Ben noted, looked out over the field at the sky beyond.

10

Ben was lying on his mattress when the phone rang. He had finished his math assignment and had just opened *Lord of the Flies* when he heard his mother say, "Jim, it's for you."

He listened to his stepfather pull himself up off the car seat in the living room on the other side of his bedroom wall. *Rescue 911* blared from the black-and-white TV, competing with the buzz of interference that periodically rippled across the screen. They couldn't afford cable and the only other channel the television would bring in was the CBC station that aired a news program at the same time. Rankin hated the news.

"Hello?" The kitchen phone was no more than six paces from Ben's doorway, and Rankin's deep voice sounded like it was in the room. Even the television was diminished by it.

Ben reached into the milk crate for his response log and a pen, then began reading the first paragraph.

"No, it ain't too late to call."

Ben glanced at the time — 9:15. Usually the foreman at the elastic plant phoned about shift changes by suppertime. His stepfather had said something to his mother about possible slow-downs, though. He crossed his fingers, hoping that wasn't the reason for the call. The repair bill for the LTD had been almost two hundred dollars, and Rankin had been ugly about it since he'd picked the car up Saturday afternoon. Ben and his mother had been walking on eggshells ever since, keeping out of his way while he ranted about crooked mechanics and where the hell he was going to come up with that kind of money. That, of course, had not stopped him from picking up a case of Moosehead on the way home from the garage, nor had it stopped him from buying another one today. He had already drained his ninth bottle when the phone rang.

His stepfather snorted. "Oh, yeah, Ben's special all right."

Ben looked up from his novel.

"No, as a matter of fact he didn't say nothin' about it."

Ben's fingers tightened around the book but he was not conscious of it. He was aware only of the silence in the kitchen pierced by the tinny wail of sirens on the TV.

"No," Ben whispered. *Please. No.*

"Yeah, that's really somethin'," the sarcasm in Rankin's slurred voice probably unapparent to the person on the other end. There was a pause. Then, "Oh, he said that, did he?"

A low moan swam up and out of Ben's throat. He wanted to sit up but he couldn't move, his body skewered to the mattress by a solid shaft of fear. He felt his heart stagger in his chest. Beat. Nothing for a long moment. Beat.

"Well, he was right. We got no money for stuff like that." Rankin coughed, a sign of impatience. He was missing *Rescue 911.* "Uh huh." Beat. "We don't take charity, Mister — what'd you say your name was?" Beat. "A handout is still a handout, Lewis. Don't matter what you call it." Beat. Beat. Beat. "Yeah, well, life's fulla disappointments, ain't it?"

Ben could hear the familiar edge to Rankin's voice. Beat-beat. Beat-beat. Beat-beat.

"Look, I dunno where you get off tellin' other people how to run their lives." Beat-beat-beat-beat-beat. "Well, it sounds like that t'me. I got no more time to talk about this crap. He ain't goin' and that's that." The bell inside the phone jangled as the receiver hit the cradle. The program had cut to a commercial and a woman was talking about taking Anacin for her aches and pains. A part of Ben's brain registered that and he grimaced. There wasn't enough Anacin in the world.

This was the part he hated most of all. The

silence just before the explosion. An image of a burning fuse flashed across his mind, Wile E. Coyote caught in a trap he'd set for the Road-runner. The cartoon character blew again and again at the end of the hissing cord. He was still blowing as his charred body hurtled skyward.

"Ben." It was a question and a command all rolled into one.

"Yes?" His voice cracked as he said it, surprising him. He didn't think he could speak at all.

There was no response. There was no need. He willed himself off the mattress, manipulated his legs until they carried him to the kitchen.

His stepfather was still standing by the phone, his big hand on the receiver. He didn't look up, just stood there waiting. Ben could smell the beery cloud even from there.

Ben's mother sat at the table, near the phone, her face a road map of lines. In her hands were Rankin's workpants she'd been mending before the call came. A threaded needle swung from a patch on the knee. Her eyes darted between her husband and her son, husband, son, husband, an invisible tennis match in progress.

Ben spoke first, his tongue a thick wad of cotton. "I told him I didn't want to go. I told him twice."

Rankin gazed at the phone as another siren shrilled in the living room. "Sounds like you told him quite a bit," he said softly.

Ben's fingernails bit deeply into the soft meat of his palms. "I said we couldn't afford it." He could hear the old Kenmore thudding in the basement beneath his feet, then realized it wasn't the washer. The sound came from inside him. Could his mother hear it? He looked at her and was sure she could.

"You're a liar." Rankin's hand left the phone and came to rest on his hip, his thumb hooked over the waist of his pants. He wavered a bit, his red eyes taking a moment to focus on Ben.

Ben looked at that hand and swallowed. His eyes could see nothing else. "I didn't lie —" he began, that hand filling the room.

"Liar," and the hand moved slightly. Almost imperceptibly. But Ben knew it had moved. Knew where it was heading. Slowly, but heading there all the same.

"Jim," Ben's mother said quietly.

His eyes flickered over her — "You shut up!" — then back to Ben. "You told him you wanted to go."

"Not at first." He saw the hand drift, a glimmer of movement along Rankin's waist. "I just wanted him to leave me alone. I didn't know what I was saying."

"You talked about me." Rankin's voice was low and emotionless — he could have been talking about the weather or underarm deodorant. His hand moved deliberately, sliding all the way around to the buckle of his belt. "You know I don't like it when you talk about me."

"Jim, please." Ben's mother started to get up but Rankin's other hand shoved her down into the chair. She hit the seat hard, but she made no sound.

Ben was blowing at Wile E.'s fuse, all the while knowing he and the coyote were on the same hopeless track. The only difference was that the next frame always showed the coyote as good as new. "I didn't say anything. I just said —"

But by now the belt — a cheap leather version of the snake in Sadie's poem — was out and there was nothing else to say.

"I won't stand for no liars in my house," Rankin said quietly. He coiled the belt around his fist then let it fall free, unwinding as it rolled into air. "Come here."

His mother's voice was even, almost natural, but he could hear beneath it the polished edge of her fear. "Ben, go to your room. Jim, there's no ne —"

Rankin's fist caught her below her left eye and her chair upended on the linoleum.

Ben saw his mother's head bounce as it hit the floor and something inside him let go. "NO!" he screamed, swinging out at his stepfather, catching the end of the belt and jerking it free of Rankin's surprised hands. Without thinking, he swung it over his head in a wide arc, intent only on getting to his mother. But the buckle of the belt, as if hungry for promised flesh, sliced through the air into Rankin's temple. The big man roared drunkenly, stumbled back against the cupboard and went down, the sound like logs released from a truck.

Ben looked down at his stepfather, blood already welling up out of the gash, then looked at the belt in his hand. His fingers jerked open as if bitten and the belt fell to the floor. The buckle made a dull ringing sound as it hit, and then Rankin roared again.

"I'll kill you!" he shouted, trying to push himself up, but his arms on the worn linoleum slid out from under him. "I'll kill you!" he raged again.

Ben glanced at his mother. Her eyes were wide — she'd turned to look at Rankin on the floor beside her, and now she turned to her son. "Go, Ben," she pleaded. When he hesitated, she cried, "I'm okay! Just go!"

He fled.

* * * *

His legs trembled as he stood gasping in the darkness. He thought of that other run he had made only four days earlier and of where it had taken him. He thought of Shay Phillips, who was probably flipping through fifty channels in his house-sized living room, already psyched for his track-and-field events the next morning. I'd have beaten you tonight, Shay, he thought. No contest.

The heat of the day had dissipated and a cool breeze riffled his clothes. Ben hadn't had time to grab a jacket, and now he shivered uncontrollably in the darkness and his teeth began to chatter. He knew, of course, that it wasn't just the temperature of the air that made him feel so cold. It was the knowledge of what he had done, of what was waiting for him back there when he returned. And, of course, it was the knowledge that his mother was *still* there. Try as he might while he ran, he'd not been able to stop the seven years of images that had flooded his mind: the shoves, the slaps, the fists punching the air from his mother's lungs, the fingers around her neck that all but robbed her of consciousness. An endless tableau of violence painted in black and white and red.

But the horror of seeing was somehow less than the horror of imagining what he wasn't there to witness. And so he'd run faster, farther, trying to outrun the movie his mind made about what had happened in that North Street bungalow after he'd left. He could only hope he'd hurt Rankin badly enough to make it too painful for him to vent his rage on his mother.

He had run with no thought of direction and, when he finally stopped, he'd found himself in front of the entrance to Memorial Park that bordered the Annapolis River. In the dim light of the streetlamp — thanks to municipal budget cuts, every other lamp was unlit — he could just make out the park's name stretched across the wrought-iron archway. Below it in smaller letters were the words "Closed from Dusk to Dawn." He wondered about the capital Ds in that message, wondered why the writer had thought those two times of day had capital-letter significance. Mentally, he put the letters back to back and came up with a zero — an adequate assessment of his life to that moment.

He passed under the entrance, the muscles in his legs already tightening, complaining, and moved deeper into the park. Down by the river, protected by the trees that lined the water's edge, there was less breeze and he found a patch of grass that was not too damp. He knelt on one knee, then the other, slowly stretching out his legs, gradually feeling the tightness leave him. Bending and twisting in the darkness, he wished there was an exercise that could as easily erase the memory of his mother's head hitting the floor, bouncing once. He knew he would remember that always.

But, of course, there were other memories just as indelible and he couldn't keep them from replaying inside his head. Like the night years earlier when Rankin destroyed the treasured books Joanne Leonard had given Ben when they'd left Edgartown. Crying, he'd tried to pull them from the fire his stepfather had built in the backyard, but Rankin had "slapped some sense into him" while his mother had stood silent, one hand gripping her side.

And there were others, the places and situations different but the role of his mother the same: mute witness to the violence she was powerless to stop. The first few times he'd hated his mother for doing nothing, then hated her for making the excuses he pretended to believe. It had taken him a while to understand the reason for her silence, but not nearly as long to realize that the hot wash of emptiness he felt wasn't hatred but hopelessness.

Well, she'd done something tonight, sure enough, but that familiar emptiness still billowed inside him, more palpable than ever before. It was useless for her to defy her husband. Rankin had proven that to her yet again this evening. Had proven it to Ben, too.

He finished stretching and sat with his knees pulled up to his chest, his arms wrapped around his shins. For the first time that day, he was grateful for his long sleeves, that afforded some warmth against the now-diminishing breeze. He looked out over the water, swathes of glass-like stillness here and there amid the ripples. The river was not wide here — no more than a baseball diamond across — but it caught and reflected the stars that stretched endlessly above him. Away from the glow of buildings and streetlights, he could make out several constellations and the gauzy ribbon of the Milky Way. He recalled reading once that a person standing in a very deep hole could see the same stars in the middle of day. If that were true, he thought bitterly, *I should be able to see them always.*

He shivered again, gooseflesh marching across his body in a hard wave, and he thought of Ann hours away surrounded by her aunt's plaid wallpaper. Even if she were home he couldn't have gone to her. Her mother barely knew him, thought of him only as "Ann's friend from school" who had been to their condominium just once. He had seen the way she'd looked at his clothes, the way she'd responded to his answer about where he lived, and he had not wanted to go back. And Ann, who was so unlike her mother, had understood. Why, then, did she no longer seem to understand the need for secrecy? Was it only that morning she'd nearly called the RCMP? Had even begged *him* to call?

He hugged his knee against him tighter trying to push back the cold. No, he couldn't call the police, especially now. He'd struck Rankin with his own belt. No police officer would side with a teenager who had attacked a parent. And whatever Rankin had done to him before would be nothing compared to what he'd do after those police left. And then, of course, he wold make them leave Brookdale. And Ann. Ben had only to think of his last night in Rockport to be sure of that.

But he had to do something. He could not go back and just take what was waiting for him. Somehow he had to convince his mother to elave the man who beat them. Somehow he had to make her see the two of them could survive without Jim Rankin. They'd done it before in Edgartown. They cold do it again. They had to.

He looked up at the stars and suddenly found himself wondering if the man who had taken that picture of his mother, the man who had deserted them both, was somewhere looking up at those same points of light. And then, even before he knew it, he was crying — soundlessly, just as Rankin had first taught him a lifetime ago.

11

"Sleep well?"

"Um," Ann mumbled as she trudged into her aunt's kitchen. Its walls were covered in paper that looked like Black Watch tartan, and it was not the most soothing sight first thing in the morning. If you looked at it long enough it seemed to vibrate, and it made Ann feel like she was trapped inside a kilt worn by a drunken highland dancer.

"Juice?" her aunt asked.

Ann nodded. Actually what she wanted was coffee, but her mother didn't approve of her drinking it and Ann didn't want to go through the silent suffering stare routine this morning. Despite what she'd indicated to Aunt Phyllis, she hadn't slept well at all. She'd tossed and turned all night long, starting at every sound in the street below her window. Halifax was noisier than Brookdale and, lying sleepless amid the chorus of car horns, squealing tires, and the occasional siren, she'd asked herself yet again why her mother couldn't have chosen an orthodontist in Brookdale, or even in Kentville or New Minas. Of course, she already knew the answer — not the standard line her mother gave her about "nothing but the best for my girl," though. The truth of the matter was that these regular checkups in the city afforded her mother the opportunity to keep abreast of the latest fashions. Clothing was everything to Ann's mother. Which was why she'd nearly had a stroke the one time Ann had brought Ben home.

Aunt Phyllis, on the other hand, was the opposite of her sister. She cared very little about what she wore as long as it was clean and comfortable. And bright. She loved great splashes of primary colours, which also explained her taste in furniture and wall coverings. Much of what she owned and wore came from thrift shops and bargain basements and she could not understand people who threw out perfectly good clothing simply because it was two hours out of style. More than once she'd teased Ann's mother for buying yet another "trendy piece of trash," and Ann's mother had simply sighed and rolled her eyes in Ann's direction as if to apologize for the "family philistine." Ann knew Ben would love Aunt Phyllis.

"I'm frying eggs and bacon," Aunt Phyllis said. "Want some?"

Ann almost said yes, if for no other reason than to see her mother react to the sight of her wallowing in all that cholesterol — besides being fanatical about fashion, she was also a fitness freak. But Ann preferred dry cereal to bacon and eggs anyway. "No thanks, Aunt Phyl. I'll just get myself some Corn Flakes."

She reached into the cupboard and pulled down the biggest box of Corn Flakes she'd ever seen. Her aunt had joined the Price Club that spring, and now her condiments, cleaning supplies, and — it would appear — her Corn Flakes came in one size only: gargantuan. Aunt Phyllis had taken Ann and her mother to the discount warehouse the afternoon before and Ann had been overwhelmed by the size of the store and the volume and variety of its products. Gaping at all that merchandise, she'd wondered what Ben would have thought of it.

Ben had been on Ann's mind since she'd said goodbye to him the afternoon before. He was, of course, the real reason she hadn't slept well — she kept picturing in her mind how upset he'd been after his meeting with Mr. Lewis, kept hearing their argument on the soccer field over and over. She'd tried to think of other memories, happier memories like the evening they'd met. She had loved Ben from that very first night in front of the library. Something about the way he stood rooted in the darkness, the way he'd said her name and watched her face when she spoke, made her feel as though she were the only person on the planet. She'd not thought it possible to love a person as much as she loved Ben.

Now she wondered if she loved him too much. After all, she hadn't been acting with the common sense everyone — except her parents — said she possessed. Common sense had been screaming at her for weeks to tell someone about Ben's stepfather. She'd looked at the "It shouldn't hurt to be a kid" poster in the drugstore so often she was sure she could produce from memory every stroke of the artist's black-and-white sketch of a bruised child on his knees. Each time she'd passed it, she'd felt she could see Ben's face in that sketch. Something about the way the artist had drawn the eyes. Looking down, looking away. Eyes that saw only pain. Never possibility.

But, she'd reminded herself, Ben wasn't a child. He was a young man. A young man who had learned to survive what surely would have destroyed others, a young man who had again begged for her silence, a young man who had told her as they'd said goodbye the day before, "Everything will be all right."

Crunching her Corn Flakes in that impossible kitchen, she wondered what Ben was doing that very moment. More important, she wondered why she felt so uneasy, as if she really didn't believe everything was going to be all right after all.

* * * *

The LTD was gone. Ben had made sure of that before he'd jumped the ditch that separated North Street from the railway line that once ran through the valley. The tracks had been pulled up years ago, but the line was still a thoroughfare for cyclists and three-wheelers and the occasional drunk looking for a shortcut to the liquor store. Ben, his body stiff from his night on the grass, had come back from the park along that line to avoid running into people on the street, but so far he'd met three early-morning joggers and an old man walking what looked to be an even older Pomeranian. Ben had kept his head down but it turned out he hadn't had to worry about anyone talking to him — the joggers wore Walkmans and the old man seemed too distressed about the dog's bowel habits to notice him: "Poo-poo, Cleo," he'd repeated again and again as Ben hurried by. "Please poo-poo, dear."

Slipping across the yard and up the back steps, he paused a moment just to be certain Rankin was not there. It would be so like his stepfather to hide the car and wait for Ben to come home, although he was pretty sure that wasn't the case — the morning shift at the elastic plant started at 7:00 and it was already 7:09. Rankin couldn't afford to be docked time, regardless of how much he might want to welcome Ben home. He'd drunk most of his last paycheque, and the rent and phone bill were both due at the end of the week.

Peering in the kitchen window Ben felt a surge of relief as he saw his mother at the sink, her back to him as she washed the breakfast dishes. He wondered what she and Rankin had had to eat since they'd finished the oatmeal the morning before. At least they'd had something, though. Another of his mother's miracles. He waited a moment longer. Then, satisfied she was alone, he opened the door.

His mother whirled about. "Ben!" she cried, crossing the kitchen in three steps and throwing her arms around his neck. "I was so worried! Where were you?"

He took hold of her arms and gently pulled them away, forcing her to step back. She knew what he was doing and turned away but he took her chin between his thumb and forefinger and turned her face towards him. "Christ," he whispered.

She seemed to frown at his choice of words, but it was an unnatural movement that reminded him of Sadie in the morning. The reason for the unnaturalness was clear: pain. It apparently gripped her face when she did more than move her lips. The flesh beneath her left eye was swollen and blotchy red, and on her cheekbone was the thin skin of a scab that had formed over a small diagonal cut. Ben knew intimately the transmutation that would occur in the next few days: the marks on his mother's face would blossom into blackness, slowly turn a reddish-brown, then eventually become yellow and fade away. He had watched the birth and bloom of these angry flowers many times, if not on his mother then in the bathroom mirror. "Christ," he whispered again.

"Ben, you know how that language upsets me," she said quietly, averting her face again.

"Does it?" The resignation he'd felt in the park last night and the relief he'd felt at the window moments earlier vanished. Anger crept into his voice like a cancer. "Is that all that upsets you?"

She looked at him as though from across a chasm. "What are you talking about?" she asked, wincing as she formed the question.

"My words upset you but you completely ignore what his fists do."

She looked at him for a long moment, a hand fluttering like a wounded bird to her face and then, self-consciously, to her side. "I'm not ignoring it," she said finally.

"Of course you are," Ben said. "That's exactly what you're doing."

"I shouldn't have interfered. If I'd kept quiet last night —"

"*You're* not the one who did anything wrong! Why can't you *see* that?"

She looked down. He knew she was looking at the ring on her left hand. "Ben, he's my husband."

"That could be changed."

She glanced up at him sharply. "And that would make everything better?"

"It certainly couldn't be worse."

She looked at him for several seconds as if meeting him after a long absence, as if searching his face for the person she thought she knew. Finally, "You've forgotten, haven't you?"

"Forgotten what?"

"What it was like. After your father left. What it was like with no food, no place to live. Nothing."

He saw her again in the kitchen of their Shank's Harbour tenement, stirring ketchup and water in a pot on the propane burner. "I haven't forgotten," he said softly.

"Yes, you have," she whispered. "Or you'd remember that was worse." She looked away, out the window towards the lumberyard where soon men and machines would begin to make their noise. "I almost turned the gas on myself that last night."

Ben's eyes widened.

She turned to him again. "Yes, God help me, it's true. You were sitting on my lap and your stomach was grumbling and I had nothing to fill it, no one to turn to. Everyone had deserted me. My parents, your father. Everyone." She paused and he could see the muscles in her throat working. Finally, "Do you know what kept me from doing it?" she asked. He didn't have to answer.

"The thought of leaving you behind, like I'd been left." She put a hand on his arm and squeezed it. "Ben, that's the very worst thing. Being left behind, being thrown away like garbage. As bad as it gets here, I know Jim's coming home each night. As much as he drinks, I know the bills will get paid." She shrugged, her hand dropping limply to her side. "Most of them, anyway. At least the ones that make the difference between sleeping on a bed or in the back of a car."

Ben stared at her, trying to see in his mind the young woman who'd made a choice between ketchup and a propane stove. "And that's enough for you?"

"Ben —"

"He treats you like garbage every day! Why can't you see that?"

"He loves me, Ben. In his own way," she added, and he could see in her eyes the look that frightened him most of all, that look of quiet resignation. He wanted to shake her.

"His own way," Ben sneered. "Look at those marks on your face! That's not love! Not anything like it!"

"You know what I told you about his own father —"

"That doesn't make it right! It can't! If anything, it makes it even more wrong. He *knows* what this feels like!"

She looked away.

A truck rumbled by the house and turned into the lumberyard, its frame creaking under the weight of logs Ben couldn't see but knew were there. There were so many things he couldn't see but knew existed nonetheless. Like Ann's love for him and his for her. Like the place inside his head where his writing came from. Like the certainty he was lucky to be alive that moment. He'd seen Rankin's eyes blazing up at him from the floor and heard the fury in his voice as he'd screamed, "I'll kill you!" He'd meant it.

By now, of course, Rankin had sobered and

cooled off, and would merely give Ben a "tuning up," as he called it. And, oh, what a special tuning it would be after last night.

But Ben had been tuned and tuned and tuned. Finely tuned for far too long. Looking at his mother, hearing the submission in her voice, he knew he would not let Rankin use his hands on him again. Could not.

Finally, Ben turned his face away in disgust. "Would you rather those marks were on *my* face?" he asked.

The sound she made was foreign to him, and her hand struck him without warning, the slap ringing about the kitchen like the report of lake ice cracking at night.

Ben's face stung, but it hurt less than the part that tore suddenly inside him. His mother had never hit him before. Not even when he was a child, long before Rankin had come into their lives, even before the man behind the camera had left them like discarded clothing, old items unfit for further use. His mother had never hit him before.

She looked at him, at the hand that had slapped him, then back at him again. "Ben —" she began.

But by then he was gone, the glassless storm door dangling ajar like the wing of a great broken bird.

* * * *

Ben shut his locker, threaded the steel "U" of the combination lock through the hasp, then spun the numbered dial. Around him voices ebbed and swelled, a meaningless babble that surged up and down the crowded hallway like the white-capped breakers he'd watched in Rockport's harbour a million years ago. People clanged locker doors, dropped books on the grey tiles, smacked and snapped wads of bubblegum, all the while calling to one another, laughing, filling the air with their casual words. Ben, of course, stood with his face towards his locker, a part of — yet apart from — the activity around him. He'd come here because it was the only place he could go.

After running from the house, he'd wandered the woods behind North Street for over an hour, eventually finding himself down by the swamp that Riley Grangeford and his family had lived beside so many years. Their house was even smaller than Ben's, empty now and windowless, one wall on the swamp side leaning in. Ben wondered if Riley ever walked down this way and looked at the life he'd left behind. Then he recalled what Sadie had said — "He asked if they would mind" — and knew, as he'd always known, that no one left anything behind. His own life was proof of that.

Emptiness ballooned in his belly and he'd thought about going to Sadie's for a slice of her bread but he didn't. There would be too many questions to answer and, besides, she'd be wrestling with her snake. Hungry, stiff, his clothes grass-stained and damp from the night before, he'd had no other choice — there had been only the school, just as there always had been only the school. As much as kids complained about teachers and homework and stupid rules and the impossible bureaucracy of lists and forms and files, it was always there, always the same, a great grey constant in a world of change. Even the rebels who regularly earned suspensions could be seen loitering on the edge of the school grounds Monday to Friday, outsiders looking in. A few of them, of course, had drugs to sell. But most were there because this was their refuge, their asylum, their hiding place when the world got too real. It was Neverland and Rod Serling's Night Gallery all rolled into one. There really was no place else.

For Ben, though, it was something more. Each of the schools he'd attended, large and small, afforded him the sense of normalcy, the anonymity he craved. For six hours each day he wasn't Jim Rankin's stepson. For six hours he was just Ben Corbett, known to teachers as the student who always had his homework done and done well; known to classmates as the shy kid who sat as close to the back of every room as he could get; unknown to principals except at the closing ceremonies in June when writing awards and prizes for highest standing in English were handed out. How he hated June and the season it heralded. Two months of heat and humidity inside long-sleeved shirts; of endless days spent alone or, if he was lucky, working at odd jobs that kept him out of Rankin's way; of learning how to be everywhere and nowhere depending on his stepfather's mood and sobriety. At night he would lie atop the sheet on his mattress longing for invisibility or September. Summer seemed four years long.

"Hey, Ben."

Ben looked up from the lock he was still holding to see Shay Phillips standing beside him. He wore a Nike warm-up suit Ben suspected cost nearly as much as the repair bill for Rankin's LTD and a Blue Jays World Series ball cap pulled down so the brim was nearly parallel with his nose. And sunglasses. Ben couldn't see Shay's eyes behind them, but that was fine with him. He could imagine the mockery they reflected. This was the moment Ben had known would come, had been dreading for five days. Now it was here.

"Hi, Shay," Ben said carefully and looked down again. He spun the dial twice to the right, pretending he'd just gotten to his locker.

There was a moment when Ben thought — hoped — that would be it, that Shay would move off to one of the groups that had formed up and down the hallway. Then, "Gonna be another hot one," Shay said.

So that was how he was going to play it. Ben thought of Sadie's cat Elijah who, much to Sadie's chagrin, toyed with each mouse he caught before killing it. Ben nodded, opening the metal door and rummaging inside for nothing. When he'd turned over every book, Shay was still there. Ben could feel his pulse flutter behind his right eye and he rubbed the back of his hand over it. Finally, he said, "I don't envy you running in that heat today."

Shay looked at his feet and Ben could see his Converse sneakers were perfectly laced, the loops of the bows equal in size. For some reason that bothered him even more than what Shay was doing right now. He shut the door of the locker harder than he needed to and the clang echoed along the hallway. "Good luck today," he said, turning away.

"Ben, about last Friday," Shay said.

Ben kept walking.

"Ben?"

Ben kept his eyes on the exit at the end of the hall. He could make it in five seconds if he ran, but he forced himself to walk normally. He wouldn't give Shay the satisfaction of seeing him run.

There were footsteps behind him. "Ben? My father shouldn't —"

"Look, I'm sorry, okay? I shouldn't have been sitting on your lawn. It was a mistake. Believe me, it won't happen again." The exit door was only a few paces away. Then the hand was on his shoulder, tugging at him. "I just wanted to say —"

Everything was white and he couldn't breathe. He spun around, his own hands flailing the air. *He asked if they would mind!* "Leave me the hell alone, okay?"

His right hand suddenly became a fist and struck Shay with a glancing blow on the chest. Surprised, Shay threw up his arms, his right hand knocking his sunglasses and Blue Jays cap off his head. He caught the glasses before they struck the floor, but the cap slid across the tiles into a group of three girls who had turned to stare at them.

Ben watched as Shay dove to retrieve it, then looked at his hand, clenched and ugly, so much like the fists his stepfather used against him again and again. He felt suddenly sick. "I'm sorry, Shay —" he began, then stopped.

Shay was already striding away from him towards the same exit Ben had been heading for only moments before. But it wasn't Shay's retreating back that had silenced Ben. It was the face he'd turned away at the last moment. A face that bore the yellowing flower of a fading bruise just below his right eye.

12

"Hey Lewis!"

Mark Lewis stopped at the guidance office doorway and turned to see Stan Patterson churning down the hall. Patterson was huge — he looked more like a professional weightlifter than a math teacher — and he dwarfed the students who stepped aside to let him pass. As he strode closer, Lewis braced himself.

"I didn't see you yesterday, Lewis. How was the camping trip?" Patterson always spoke at full volume as though shouting over loud music, and Lewis saw several students turn amused eyes in their direction.

"Not bad, Stan."

"Poured like a monsoon here all weekend,"

thundered Patterson.

"It rained at Keji, too."

"Must've been miserable!"

"Not really. There's still plenty to do when it rains."

"Can't imagine being in a tent. Give me a hotel room any day!" Patterson boomed.

Lewis smiled thinly. He and Patterson had had this same conversation half a dozen times in the past, and he'd given up trying to convince the math teacher that camping wasn't an act of insanity. He glanced at his watch: only a few minutes before he had to be in homeroom. "Stan, I've got to run. See you later." And he stepped into the guidance office.

Marie Comeau, the guidance counsellor, was talking on the phone. "Just need to check a file," he said softly.

She gestured towards the wall of cabinets behind her and kept talking.

He found the cabinet containing the records of the current eleventh-graders, opened the drawer with "11-C" on it, and thumbed through several folders until he found the one he was after. He pulled it out and rolled the drawer shut. "I'll bring this back today," he said, showing her the name on the folder: CORBETT, BEN.

She nodded and he left.

Back in his classroom, he sat down at his desk and began flipping through the file. It was the first time he'd seen it. While some of his colleagues routinely read their classes' files at the beginning of each school year to determine strengths and weaknesses of individual students, Mark Lewis preferred not to look at them unless he found it necessary. He liked forming his own impressions of students rather than being influenced by comments and assessments made by other teachers and administrators and, in many cases, psychologists and social workers. If, in the course of a school year, he felt he needed to know more about a student's learning profile or personal background, then he would go to those files. This was one of those times.

He regretted having called Ben's stepfather last night. He shouldn't have interfered. Money was obviously more of a problem for that family than he'd imagined, and he'd only underscored it by offering what Mr. Rankin had interpreted as charity. He hoped he hadn't offended Ben as well.

He'd tossed and turned most of the night, upset with having handled the situation so badly. For the first time, he realized how naive he was. Just because his students wrote and shared and discussed each day in his classroom did not mean he knew them, knew who they were when they walked out that door. He saw them forty-five minutes each day. There was a lot of that day left that he knew nothing about.

And so he'd gotten out of bed intending to learn more about Ben Corbett. Once at school, he'd gone to the staffroom and spoken to a few of Ben's other teachers, some who taught him this year and a couple who'd taught him most of the previous one, but no one had more to say than "good student" and "kind of quiet." Now here he was with his file. Lewis shook his head sadly. Everything came down to files.

The only thing in Ben's records that surprised him was the number of schools the boy had attended. Aside from that, there was nothing unusual, nothing the teacher didn't already know. Excellent performance at the elementary level; good marks in all of his secondary courses, some outstanding ones in a few. A couple of comments about absenteeism — "Would perform even better with regular attendance" — but not a single notation about behavioural problems or difficulties with other students. He had never been sent to the office, had never skipped a class. Everything was as the teacher had expected. Still, Lewis couldn't shake the feeling that he was missing something, that something was not as it should be.

The 8:55 warning bell bonged over the PA, and students began pouring into the classroom. The teacher closed the file folder and stood up, greeting each one of them by name.

* * * *

Most of Ben's classes were a waste of time. Several of his classmates were track-and-field athletes and many, like Shay, had qualified for the district competitions in Lakewood. With so many students away, teachers were reluctant to continue with new work they'd only have to repeat the next day —

most of them gave their classes time to catch up on homework assignments Ben had already done. But he went to all of them. Except English. He couldn't face Mr. Lewis after the things Rankin had said to him on the phone and he'd spent third period across the street at Needs Convenience Store browsing through magazines. It was a poor choice of places to hide out — the smell of fresh doughnuts and coffee only made him more conscious of his empty stomach.

By the time the last bell of the day rang, he felt nauseated. He had gone much longer in the past without something to eat, but the confrontation with Rankin the night before and the episodes that morning with his mother and Shay had taken their toll. As he walked across the parking lot, he hoped he'd find something in the cupboard when he got home. There'd be time to worry about everything else later.

As he reached the end of the parking lot, two cars pulled up beside him, then turned right onto the street. A third rumbled up and stopped. Its driver tapped the horn and Ben turned to see Mr. Lewis's ancient Camaro beside him, the splatter of red lead on its doors and fenders similar to the patchwork Rankin had painted on the LTD. At least Rankin's red lead appeared to be covering something; several students had laughingly told Mr. Lewis that the rust-inhibitor actually seemed to be holding his car together. The teacher had not disagreed.

"Hello, Ben," Mr. Lewis said, leaning out the

driver's side window. "Need a lift?"

Red-faced, Ben shook his head. "Thanks anyway. I don't have far to go." He felt as though he should say more. "I like to walk," he added.

The teacher smiled. "So do I," he said. "I don't even mind that long walk between my room and the vice-principal's office." He smiled again, even more broadly. "Speaking of the vice-principal, how do you suppose Mr. Baxter feels about people who skip classes?"

Ben looked at his feet, wondering if the words "complete fool" were written across his forehead.

"Sure you couldn't use a ride?" Mr. Lewis asked again.

Ben looked up. "I guess maybe I could after all," he replied.

"Good." Mr. Lewis leaned over to open the passenger's door.

Ben came around the car and slid into the worn bucket seat. While not corroded with rust, the interior of the car wasn't in much better shape than the exterior. Large cracks yawned in the plastic dash and several seams in the upholstery had let go exposing yellowed foam. The once-blue fabric overhead dangled to eye level in the back seat and there was no handle on the door behind Mr. Lewis.

The teacher noticed Ben's observations. "I know. She should be condemned. That's what my wife says, anyway. But she was my first car." He patted the steering wheel. "I haven't been able to part with her." He moved the stick shift ahead to first gear and eased the car towards the street. "Which way?"

Ben thought quickly. "Left," he replied, ignoring the ball of air in his belly. "I'm going to the library." There was no way he'd let the teacher see where he lived. The motor rumbled throatily as the car swung into the street.

"Are you okay, Ben?" Mr. Lewis asked.

Ben didn't know what he meant, tried a dozen answers in his mind, then settled on the shortest. "Sure."

The teacher glanced over at him, then back at the road. "I don't want there to be a problem between us. You've never skipped my class before. In fact, I know you've never skipped anyone's class. I checked."

Ben flushed and looked out the open window at the parked cars and buildings they passed. He groped for an apology that wouldn't sound insincere. He certainly didn't want there to be a problem between them either.

"I'm sorry," Mr. Lewis said.

Ben blinked at him. "What?"

"I never should have called your stepfather. I told you I'd accept your decision about not going to Ottawa but then I went ahead and called anyway. I know you're upset with me and you deserve to be. I'm sorry. But I want you back in my class."

Ben looked at the teacher, amazed. "No," he said. "*I'm* the one who's sorry." He paused, trying to hear what the words sounded like before he said them. "I was ashamed of how he treated you on the phone. I just didn't want to face you today."

The teacher looked over at him and smiled again. "Don't worry about that. I've been treated a whole lot worse by parents with sharper tempers than his."

Ben doubted it, but he said nothing. They'd turned down Gates Avenue and he could see the library up ahead and he was almost disappointed. He appreciated the teacher's efforts to make things right between them. He'd never heard a man say he was sorry before.

"Anyway," continued Mr. Lewis as he clicked on the turn indicator, "I just wanted you to know I've learned my lesson. No more pressure about that Summer Institute." As he pulled to a stop in front of the library, the Camaro sputtered and he jazzed the accelerator until the engine evened out. "And I want to see you fifth period tomorrow, all right?"

"Yes, sir."

"No hard feelings?"

Ben shook his head.

"Good," the teacher said, sticking out his hand to shake his student's.

The movement surprised Ben and he instinctively pulled back, bumping his shoulder on the door. The teacher sat with his hand extended and looked at Ben with narrowed eyes. Ben fumbled for the door handle.

"Ben?"

"Yeah?" he replied, his hand pulling on the handle. Nothing happened. The door wouldn't open.

"Is anything wrong?"

"No. Nothing's wrong." But he knew he'd said it too fast, too loud. He could feel the teacher's eyes on him, perhaps noticing for the first time the grass stains on his shirt, his sleeves buttoned at the cuff despite the heat of the day. He tried the handle again, and again the door did not open.

"Ben, did anything happen after I called last night?"

"No," he said. He pulled again. Nothing. Panic rose inside him. "How do you get out of here?" he demanded. By now he was yanking the handle back and forth, back and forth, and a warning sounded at the base of his brain. *BE ALERT! BE ALERT!*

"Ben, what's wrong? Why are you so upset?"

"I'm not upset!" All he could see was white, like the sun reflecting off flat snow. "I just have things to do. What's wrong with this door?"

"That handle only works a certain way. You have to know the combination." The teacher reached across, and too late Ben realized he was reaching for the handle. He flinched again, his body jerking back like a leash-yanked dog. *DamnitDamnit* he cursed, the words echoing against the inside of his skull.

The teacher sat back in his seat. The car sputtered again but he did nothing to stop it and the engine stalled, a row of red beacons lighting up the dashboard. The sudden silence was deafening.

DamnitDamnitDamnitDamn —

"Talk to me, Ben."

Ben looked out the window and took a deep

breath, forcing his empty stomach back down inside his chest. "I have to go, Mr. Lewis," he said evenly.

The teacher said nothing for a moment. A car drove by, the backwater of its passing filling the Camaro with a sudden wave of sound that ebbed slowly into silence. Then, "Did your stepfather hit you last night?"

Ben didn't turn from the window. "No, he didn't," he said. But the truth sounded like a lie even to him.

"Ben, roll up your sleeves."

Oh no oh no oh "What?"

"You heard me. Roll up your sleeves."

no oh no oh no. His brain lit up like the dash-board except, instead of being red, the lights were white and each of them had a voice whispering his name. He had to get out of there. Ben reached through the window and grabbed the rusted chrome handle outside, his thumb punching the button. Miraculously the door opened and he swung his legs out and leaned forward. He was almost out of the car when he felt the teacher's hand grab his shirt.

"Ben!" Mr. Lewis cried. "I only want to —"

And then the shirt tore. Secondhand from Frenchy's and worn thin by repeated washings, it ripped diagonally across the side and round the back, a sudden wound in the fragile cotton. It hadn't even torn at a seam.

The sound was like a gunshot inside the car and Ben's brain. *Oh no oh —*

"My God," the teacher breathed.

Ben felt himself slump back onto the seat. There was little point in running now. He knew what Mr. Lewis had seen: the week-old road map of exploded veins and discoloured skin he'd received when Rankin had thrown him through the storm door. "I fell," he said weakly, his voice almost a whisper.

"My God," the teacher repeated.

"I fall down a lot —" he continued but the teacher cut him off.

"Ben, I'm not a fool. I know what I see here."

Ben clenched his teeth to keep from screaming. "You don't know anything," he said simply.

"Then tell me, Ben." The teacher's voice was barely audible. "Tell me what I don't know."

Ben looked at the hands in his lap, hands that could push Bic pens across paper forming words as easily as shadows. Where were those words now?

"Ben, I only want to help you."

Ben looked up. "Help me?"

The teacher took a deep breath. "I imagine this has been going on for a long time, hasn't it? Does he hit your mother, too?"

Ben looked down again. His fingers locked in whitening Xs.

Mr. Lewis twisted in the bucket seat so his whole body was facing the teenager. "What's happening to you and your mother is a crime, Ben. Your stepfather is breaking the law. The police —"

"NO!" The words were suddenly there. "You can't, Mr. Lewis. Please! Not the police. Nobody!"

"Ben —"

"I can *handle* this. *We* can handle this. My mother and I. No one has to know."

The teacher's words were soft but thick, like cotton wadded into small round balls. *"I* know, Ben."

"Mr. Lewis —"

"And from the looks of that," the teacher interrupted, nodding towards Ben's shirt, "you're *not* handling it. Not at *all.*"

Ben turned away. Everything was falling apart. Like the ancient Camaro they were sitting in.

"The police have to know, Ben."

"I thought you wanted to help me," Ben whispered.

"I do."

"This won't help. You have to believe me."

The teacher said nothing for a moment. Then, "You have to believe that it will, Ben. It's the *only* thing that can help."

Another car pulled up to the curb in front of them and a tall woman in her late forties or early fifties got out. She leaned down and said something to the driver, then went into the library as the car pulled away. Watching her through the windshield, Ben felt like he was looking at life on another planet.

"Will you call them, Ben?"

Ben's eyes blurred.

"Ben?"

"Mr. Lewis —" he began, but his throat closed over his words.

The teacher waited. Finally, "Will you get your

mother to call them?".

"You —" Ben croaked, "you don't understand."

"Ben," the teacher's voice was still soft, but there was an urgency beneath his words, "I understand that he won't just stop. Not on his own. Why *should* he? People like your stepfather think they have a right to hurt their families. And they *keep* doing it unless someone makes them stop. You don't deserve this, Ben. Neither does your mother." He shook his head sadly. "I can't imagine what this has been like for you. I only wish I'd seen it sooner." He raised his hand and for a moment it hung in the air between them. Then his thumb and index finger found the bridge of his nose in a gesture he'd performed a thousand times at the front of his classroom when pondering questions posed by his students. "I understand if you can't go to the police. But I have to."

"No! Please —"

"Ben, I can't ignore this —"

"Please, Mr. Lewis!" Ben heard himself pleading, his voice sounding much like the first times he'd begged Rankin to stop. He'd soon learned, though, that pleading only made it worse. "Take it like a man!" Rankin would snarl, his fists coming down again and again. And he had.

But now he had even more to lose. Now there was Ann. "Please, don't do this."

"You're under eighteen, Ben. I'm required by law to report this." He looked again at the ripped shirt. "And even if I weren't, I would. No one should be able to do that to a person and get away with it."

Ben was almost hysterical now. "But you'll ruin everything!" he sobbed, heaving himself up off the seat. "Everything!"

"Ben! Wait!"

But by then Ben was out of the car, running faster than he'd ever run before.

13

Ann drummed her fingers on the side of the door and gritted her teeth again. The car radio was playing her favourite 10,000 Maniacs song but she barely heard it. She swivelled in the bucket seat for the hundredth time so she could see out the back window, but again it was a wasted effort. Still no sign of her mother.

"Just one more stop," her mother had said as they'd turned onto Bayers Road from Chebucto. Ann had thought they were heading towards the 102, which would take them directly out of the city, but when they'd come abreast of the Halifax Shopping Centre her mother had signalled for a left turn.

"Mother!" Ann had complained. "We've already

been to Park Lane and Spring Garden Place, and we did Scotia Square and MicMac Mall last night. I want to get home." She'd felt increasingly uneasy as the day had worn on and twice she'd almost called Ben from a phone booth. Which, of course, was pointless since Ben was still in school. And dangerous, too, since she never knew when Rankin might answer. Despite Ben's warnings, she'd phoned his house twice in the months she'd known him, once last Friday to find out about his meeting with Mr. Lewis and once the week before Christmas after he'd missed three days of school. Rankin had answered that time and she'd had to grip the receiver to keep from dropping it. His voice was thick and swollen like the Annapolis River in spring, and for a moment she'd seen before her Ben's face as he'd looked that afternoon framed by his bedroom window. "Sorry, wrong number," she'd muttered and jammed the receiver into its cradle.

She'd seen that same face before her again today, more than once. The first time, she'd been flipping through a medical journal in Dr. Shroeder's waiting room and had come across before-and-after photos of people who'd undergone radical dental surgery. The people in the "before" pictures were always unsmiling, as if they could think only about the pain that was to come. The second time, she and her mother had been stuck at a red light and she'd spied that "It shouldn't hurt to be a kid" poster on the back of a bus. Ben's face had swum up out of the exhaust that unfurled behind Halifax Transit 12, and she'd had to blink twice to make sure he wasn't really there.

Something wasn't right — she could feel it. But she couldn't tell her mother that. Or anyone else. She could only cross her fingers again and hope that everything was fine while her mother weaved in and out of traffic and, later, every shopping mall within a five-kilometre radius of Aunt Phyllis's apartment.

"The last one. I promise," her mother had said as she'd manoeuvred her strawberry Celica through the crowded parking lot. Of course, she'd said that when she'd dragged Ann through Spring Garden Place just after lunch, and Ann had no reason to believe her now.

"What could you possibly want that you haven't bought already?" Ann had demanded. The trunk was nearly filled with bags from clothing stores and accessory shops and a place called The Lady of Leather where her mother had purchased — among other things — two identical pairs of suede pumps. Her mother had assured her that one pair was peach and the other was coral, but Ann couldn't see the difference. She'd been conscious only of the gleam in the salesman's eyes as he'd rung up the grand total on her mother's Gold Visa.

"Something for the hospital auxiliary banquet next week," her mother had said as she swung the car into a parking spot for the handicapped. She never felt guilty about using those spaces and had, in fact, ranted about paying the two fines she'd received in the past for doing so. "We're all handicapped in one way or another," she'd told Ann while grudgingly writing out a cheque for the last fine. Ann had thought being divorced didn't constitute a handicap, but she knew it was pointless to tell her mother that. She'd even given up groaning every time her mother pulled into one of those spots, choosing to hunker down in her seat instead. There were some things you just couldn't change, and her mother was one of them.

Ann frowned. "I thought the satin dress you bought at Chez Noire was for that."

"No, that's for the library fund-raiser. I don't have anything for the banquet." Although she'd lived in Brookdale only eight months, Ann's mother had immersed herself in community groups and their functions. They gave her an opportunity to wear what she bought.

Ann thought about the dresses that lined the closets in her mother's bedroom and she'd wanted to scream. Instead, she gritted her teeth, her newly tightened braces like a hand across her mouth. "How long will you be?"

"Oh, not long," her mother had replied as she checked her hair and makeup in the visor mirror. "Coming with me?"

"No, Mother," she'd sighed. Maybe if she waited in the car her mother wouldn't take as long. She wouldn't be so inclined to look at clothes for Ann, too.

Ann glanced at the digital clock on the dash and turned to look out the rear window once more. Nothing. "Come ON!" she breathed between clenched teeth. She turned back again, the wheelchair logo on the sign in front of the car suddenly face-like and mocking. She thought of Ben and wondered what he was doing, wished she was with him now.

* * * *

Ben wasn't even aware he was crying. His finger jabbed the button beside the handsome oak door for the seventh time and from inside came the muted echo of chimes, but he was conscious of neither the tears on his face nor the sobs that shuddered through his body. He only knew that Ann had to be there. Had to be.

Mr. Lewis hadn't followed him. He couldn't have, anyway. Ben had run behind the library and jumped the mesh fence that separated it from the municipal building on Church Street, which ran parallel to Gates Avenue where he'd left the teacher. He'd streaked past the "Building a Better Community" sign on the lawn in front of the town hall, then crossed Church and ran south towards Riverside Drive and Ann.

As he'd run, he hadn't even considered the possibility she might not yet be home. There were too many other thoughts, too many sounds and images flashing through his mind: the threat Rankin made the evening before they'd left

Rockport, "If you ever say anythin' to anybody again . . ."; Rankin's big hands only last night sliding his belt from its loops; Rankin's huge frame crashing to the kitchen floor; Rankin roaring "I'll kill you!" over and over.

Ben thought of his mother: her face in the photograph, her face against the linoleum, her face behind the hand that had struck him only hours before. A face he no longer recognized.

Then there were the other images: his first sight of Freemont's Lumber Yard, his first day at Brookdale High, his first day at all the schools he'd ever attended, the beginnings without number that had marked the passage of his lifetime since Edgartown.

And superimposed over all these images was Ann. There could be no more new beginnings without her.

For the first few minutes his panic hadn't permitted him rational thought, but by the time he reached the walkway in front of Ann's house and bounded up the steps to her front door, he knew what he had to do. The only thing left for him to do. He would have to run.

But he could not leave without seeing her, without telling her that he was going and that he would call her when he got wherever it was that Rankin could not reach him. Somehow they would be together again. Maybe not for a while, but it would happen. It had to. Just as Ann had to be there now.

But she wasn't. He knew that now. The doorbell

chimed again as he slumped against the door frame, his face in his hands.

Then he heard the siren.

It was a long, low wail in the distance, but it was getting louder, heading towards him. Some part of his brain recalled his physics teacher describing the Doppler effect, the same phenomenon that helped explain the universe and its explosive beginnings. As Ben stood frozen on Ann's front step, his mind registering the siren and what it must mean, a similar explosion bloomed in his chest and radiated outwards in icy waves of fear. *no no No No NO*

By the time the ambulance swept by the corner of Riverside Drive and Main heading towards the accident scene on Water Street, Ben was long gone.

* * * *

Ann craned her neck over the people in front of her, scanning the crowds for a glimpse of her mother. She'd waited in the car as long as she could stand to, but the feeling that something was wrong had intensified and she could sit still no longer. She had no idea where to begin looking but she had to find her mother, had to get her in the car and on the road and headed towards home. Even as she zigzagged down the mall past Thriftys and Color Your World, she knew that somehow time was running out.

* * * *

NO!

The word clawed its way up Ben's throat and he bit his lip to keep from screaming it aloud. The LTD sat in the driveway across from Freemont's Lumber Yard. Rankin was home.

The rumour about slowdowns at the elastic plant must have been true. That was the only reason Rankin wouldn't be at work. That, or he'd been fired. Either way, he was home. And he was probably waiting for Ben.

Ben eased back into the shadow of the two-by-fours stacked along the mill's rear entrance. Running down North Street, he'd seen the bumper of a car jutting out past the corner of his house and he'd been sure it was the police. He'd cut through the lumberyard where he'd planned to wait until they left, but then he'd seen the rest of the car, had known who was really there, and fear had slivered through him, welding him to the spot.

His mind whirled. He needed clothes and some food, not just now but for later when he'd found a place. He had no idea where he was going but the weather was warmer now. He could sleep outdoors. He had done it last night and he could do it again. But food was a problem. As frightened as he was, he was hungry too, and he knew soon he'd be even hungrier. He'd need something in his stomach to keep his strength up.

He thought about Sadie, then remembered this was Wednesday, the afternoon the Baptist Women's Group met to sew quilts and hook rugs that they eventually sold on consignment at the Art Barn, the money going to their missionary fund. Sadie had once joked about a woman of her age being a hooker and Ben had laughed and laughed. Now he fought to keep from crying again.

He stood in the shadows for nearly fifteen minutes watching the house. There was no movement. Occasionally, when the whine and snarls of the saws behind him let up a bit, he could hear the sound of canned laughter and applause drift out the living room window and he knew Rankin was watching TV. He watched and listened a few minutes longer. Still nothing. Maybe Rankin was asleep. If he'd been drinking, that was a good possibility.

He waited five more minutes, his heart pounding, then stepped out of the shadow onto North Street.

* * * *

"Mother!"

Ann's mother turned around, a shopping bag dangling from each hand, and she smiled. "Ann! You decided to come in after all. I'm glad. Isn't it great?" She nodded towards dozens of "UP TO 70% OFF" banners hanging high above their heads. Her face was flushed, and a few strands of hair had come loose from her perfect ponytail. "It's some sort of anniversary sale. We couldn't have come at a better time."

"Mother, we have to go." Ann reached for one of the shopping bags and took it from her.

But her mother was already moving away from her. "Just one more store," she called over her shoulder. "I want to find a hat to go with —"

"MOTHER!"

Ann's mother wheeled around. "Ann, for goodness sake, you're not in a gymnasium. People are staring."

Ann swallowed to keep from screaming. When she spoke, her voice was even, a testament to her mother's infinite remonstrations regarding public displays of emotion. "Mother," she said, "I'm going. With or without you."

Her mother's face was a puddle of expressions, one rippling into another and yet another. "What did you say?" she asked finally.

"We have to go," Ann repeated simply. "Please, Mother."

Her mother looked at her a moment longer, seeing in her daughter's eyes more than irritation, more than impatience. She saw fear. "Why didn't you just say so?" she asked, taking Ann's arm and leading her towards the exit.

* * * *

Ben stood on the tips of his toes and, cupping his hands around his eyes, he peered through the living room window.

For nearly five minutes he'd been crouching out of sight around the corner of the house, all the while listening for any sign of movement inside. There had been none. Now he knew why. Rankin lay stretched out on the car seat by the far wall, several empty beer bottles on the floor beside him. His mouth was open and he was breathing deeply. A housefly walked across his face and his cheek flickered involuntarily, but he did not wake up.

Ben knew what he had to do. Time was running out.

He slipped around the side of the house and crept up the step, his sneakers soundless against the sagging wood. He reached over the railing and eased the clothespins off two shirts and a pair of jeans hanging from the line he had strung last year between the house and a pine tree in the backyard. Laying them on the railing, he turned to the door. Luckily, the inside door was ajar. He paused to listen again. From the living room came the collective groan of a game show audience commiserating with a losing contestant. The sound track of my life, Ben thought.

He gently pulled open the outside storm door, being careful to lift up on it so the rusted hinges would not squeak.

* * * *

Ann's mother pulled the paper out from under the driver's side windshield wiper, then unlocked the Celica's doors with the chirp of her electronic entry device. Putting the shopping bags into the back, she slid into the front bucket seat beside Ann and unrolled the paper. "At least it's not a ticket," she said.

Ann looked at her as she read it. "What is it?"

Her mother looked blandly at the sheet of paper. "A note," she said simply, crumpling it between her fingers and tossing it into the back seat.

"Who from?"

Her mother put her key into the ignition, turned it, and the Celica purred to life. "Someone with as much patience as you, it would seem," she said as she backed out of the parking space and pointed the car towards Brookdale.

"Maybe they're trying to tell you something," Ann offered, relieved to be heading home at last.

"Apparently," her mother murmured, looking both ways as she eased the car into the flow of traffic. When she'd guided the car back up onto Bayers Road and into the outbound lane leading to the 102, she continued, "And what are *you* trying to tell me?"

"What do you mean?"

Her mother glanced over at her, then returned her attention to the road. "Ann, I admit I can be a little unfocused sometimes, especially when there's a sale sign in front of me. But I'm still your mother. You've been agitated since I picked you up at school yesterday, and all you've talked about today is getting home. What's going on?"

Ann watched the cars passing them in the left lane, almost as if their Celica were stationary.

Everything moved so fast lately. Nothing ever stood still, stayed the same. Even speed limits were meant to be broken. She didn't say anything for a long while. Then, "Mother, there's something I have to tell you," she began.

* * * *

Once in the kitchen, Ben moved to the drawer by the sink and pulled out two Save-Easy bags, one for the clothes he'd taken off the line and the other for whatever food he could find. Seeing dishes in the drainer by the sink, he realized he'd need a cup and plate and at least a spoon. He took one of each from the drainer and held them carefully — he could not risk their clinking together in the bag until he was out of earshot. Then he moved to the cupboard by the stove. Opening the upper door, he found nothing inside. The lower cupboard, however, contained four cans. Two were beans in tomato sauce and a third was a tin of Clarke's Irish Stew. The fourth was a can of Hunt's spaghetti sauce, his mother's favourite. With his free hand, he eased the first three one at a time into the plastic bags he'd laid open on the floor.

He had just closed the cupboard door when Rankin grabbed him, knocking the cup, plate, and spoon from his hand.

14

Mark Lewis sat by the phone in the guidance office. Marie Comeau sat across from him.

"Do you want me to do it?" she asked.

He shook his head. "No. I should be the one." But he didn't move. Couldn't.

"You can't blame yourself for not knowing," Marie said after a moment.

"Why can't I?" He looked down at his hands numbly gripping the arms of the chrome and vinyl chair. He'd been gripping the chair ever since he'd sat down. It was the only way he could keep his hands from shaking.

"You aren't his only teacher," she said softly.

"It was in his file. The number of times he's moved." He could barely speak. All he could see was that bruise the size of a dinner plate beneath Ben's shirt.

"Lots of families move all the time. For all kinds of reasons."

"All those times he missed school." He seemed to be talking more to himself than to her.

"And every one of them explained and excused."

He ignored her. "If you could have seen his back . . ." His voice trailed off.

"Mark, he's not the only one. I see students every year who face what Ben is going through right now."

The teacher looked up. "Every year?"

"Every year."

"Jesus," he whispered.

"And those are just the ones we find out about. For every one I *do* see, who knows how many I *don't* see?"

He looked at her, his face suddenly slack like an inner tube leaking air. "How can this happen without people knowing?"

Marie reached over and put her hand on his shoulder. "The how is easy. Fear. And shame. Kids seldom want anyone to know it's happening. Would you?" She sat back in her chair. "It's the *who* and the *why* that often surprise me. No two cases are the same. There are often similar elements, similar patterns of abuse, but each situation is unique."

Lewis shook his head and gripped the chair arms even tighter. For all the assurances he'd given Ben in the car, this was all new to him. He felt like he was floundering in high surf. "He said I'd ruin everything if I told," he said quietly.

"Of course you will. All the intricate lines of defence, the checks and balances — the whole house of cards will come down. Why shouldn't he be afraid of that happening? He's known nothing else."

"Do you know Ben?"

It was her turn to shake her head. "No, just kids *like* him. To tell you the truth, when you called from the library and said you needed to talk to me about Ben, I got his file out and looked at it for the first time. Oh, I'd seen it before, put things in it like term reports and school photos, but I'd never read it."

He took a long, shuddering breath. "I should never have sent his writing away without his permission. Look at the trouble I've caused him."

"Mark, you didn't cause any of this. You were only trying to help him. Like you're trying to help him now."

He looked at the phone on her desk. "I hope I'm doing the right thing."

"It's the law, Mark. You don't have a choice."

You don't have a choice. He wondered if Ben had told himself the same thing all those years.

15

The plate shattered as it hit the floor beside the spoon. The cup, a heavy stoneware mug bought three for a dollar at Bi-Way, landed on its handle snapping it cleanly away. Unhindered by this protrusion, the cup rolled under the table and clinked against the metal leg of a chrome chair. This succession of crash, roll, and clink seemed like sound effects in a film, the action suddenly slowing to a halt until a single image hung frozen on the screen: Rankin's meaty hand wrapped around Ben's arm, holding it high in the air.

The action remained frozen a split second longer, then Rankin spun Ben around to face him. "Goin' somewheres, Benny-boy?"

Rankin's face was twisted in a parody of a smile,

his eyes moist and red. Drool glistened like snail tracks on his chin and a cloud of stale beer and body odour emanated from him. Above him a housefly dive-bombed his head, its buzzing melding with the sound of saws from the mill.

But the detail that caught and held Ben's eyes, looming over him in that tiny kitchen, was the cut on the left side of Rankin's face. He could almost see the imprint of the belt buckle where it had struck him just below the hairline.

Ben felt his bowels loosen.

The mock smile disappeared. "I asked you a *quesshun!* Are you *goin'* somewheres?" He belched without warning, the sound deep and sudden, and spittle sprayed from his mouth onto Ben's face and neck. Rankin swayed backward, then righted himself. His hand on Ben's arm was a cruel vice and he yanked it down and behind Ben's back, crushing the teenager against him.

A tearing sensation seared Ben's shoulder. He cried out, and then the smile was back. "I dint *hear* you!" Rankin slurred. He jerked his hand up under Ben's shoulder blade. "What'd you say?"

"Yes!" Ben gasped through clenched teeth. "I'm going!"

It wasn't the answer Rankin expected. His face slackened in surprise, as did his fingers on Ben's arm.

Even through the white haze of his pain and fear, Ben saw his chance. He took it. Wheeling around, he shoved backwards against Rankin's chest and simultaneously pushed down with all his strength. His arm broke free of Rankin's grip and he flung himself forward towards the kitchen door.

Rankin grunted in astonishment, reached out, and grabbed empty air.

Ben might have made it if not for the pieces of shattered plate on the floor. His sneakers crunched the cheap stoneware, which slipped frictionless across the worn linoleum, and his feet went out from under him. He fell like a stone, his right knee banging against the wall by the door.

Then Rankin was over him laughing, the sound guttural and animal-like, and Ben felt the steel toe of his stepfather's old Kodiak work boot punch into his left side, whooshing the air from his lungs. "You good-fer-nothin' —"

His epithet was lost in the roar in Ben's ears. The boot had kicked him again, this time catching Ben in the side of the head, and he yelled in pain. The room swam in front of him, black dots the size of dimes floating against the yellowed plaster. He gripped his skull between his hands to keep it from exploding and he felt something warm and wet beneath his left palm. An alarm rang raucously somewhere in the room, then he dimly realized only he could hear the sound — a strident ringing in his ears.

"Thought you could raise a hand t'me 'n' get away with it?" It was less a question than a snarl, followed by another kick, this one to Ben's shoulder. "You shoulda learnt by now what I'd do t'you if you ever raised a hand t'me."

The boot came again and this time somewhere above the ringing Ben heard a snap. But both the ringing and the snap were lost beneath the sounds of his screams. Even the rattle and whine of the saws through the open window sounded distant, mosquitoes buzzing in a darkening room.

Some part of him knew it was over. Knew this would finish it. Knew what had started could not be stopped. He wanted to shout something at Rankin, longed to scream the words he'd locked inside himself for seven long years, but blood bubbled into his mouth and he was choking.

Then he *was* shouting, screaming at Rankin to stop, threatening him if he didn't step back. But his lips weren't moving, except in the pushing, pursed motion of spitting. The only sounds he made were sobs and moans, followed by gagging coughs that set his lungs afire. The words he heard weren't his own.

Ben opened his eyes to see his mother standing in the doorway silhouetted against the May brightness. Tears rivered down her cheeks but her head was high. Out of Ben's pain came the photograph that lay hidden beneath his mattress, blurred yet corporeal. "If you touch him again," she was shouting, "I'll kill you, Jim!"

Amazingly, Rankin did step back and Ben's mother knelt beside her son. "It's okay, Ben," she whispered, her cool hands fluttering over him. She touched his face and her fingers came away red, and he heard her sob. "It's all right now."

But over her shoulder Ben saw what she

couldn't see, what he couldn't tell her through the blood in his mouth. Rankin had reached for his belt buckle, loosening it and slipping the leather length out of his pants in one fluid motion. Ben moaned and tried to raise his arm to point, but lightning ripped through him.

"Looks like I got me another one needs teachin'," Rankin said softly, and he stepped towards them. His boots crunched the broken pieces of plate like potato chips.

Ben's mother whirled to face him. "No more, Jim!" she cried jumping to her feet. "This is the end of it! I won't let you. Ever again!"

Rankin looked at her through wide, rheumy eyes. "You won't *let* me?" he repeated softly, his body swaying slightly. He looked down at Ben. "She won't *let* me, Benny-boy," and he chuckled, the sound like water moving slow but deep. There were things moving around in that water, down in the dark places where the light didn't reach.

Rankin looked at his wife and smiled, his teeth a yellow rupture in his stubbled face. "Oh, I'm gonna enjoy this," he said, stepping closer. "You're as bad as that boy of yours."

Ben's mother grabbed the chair Rankin had knocked over the night before with her in it and she swung it back and forth in front of her, the legs pointing at Rankin. "You get back, Jim!" she shouted. "You leave us alone!"

Ben tried to sit up, but pain razored through him and he fell back, gasping.

"Oh, I'll leave you alone," Rankin grunted,

moving unsteadily towards her. He belched again, the sound like an eruption in the tiny room. "I'll leave you *both* alone. Just as soon as I teach you a little *respect*." He folded the leather belt over on itself twice, then smacked it against the palm of one hand. "Hear that?" he asked softly. "Get used to the sound."

Then he was on her, the chair crashing against the kitchen wall. Ben's mother went down, her arms flailing helplessly against Rankin's bulk.

Ben screamed and he felt something tear inside. But the sound didn't stop. It kept building and building, rising up over them on great white wings, filling the room, the house, the street. It shrilled and wailed, clamoured and clung to them, lifted them up out of themselves and flung them forward into darkness.

16

"Phone, Ben."

Ben looked up from the fat duotang he'd been scribbling in only moments earlier. "Thanks, Julie," he said, easing himself up off the bed.

The girl in the doorway nodded. She was about ten, but her slight size made her seem much younger. It wasn't until you looked in her eyes that you realized how old she actually was — which Ben sometimes thought was a hundred. Julie Hennesey had lived two lifetimes already, both marred by fists and fear. "How's it going?" she asked quietly, her words like feathers in the air.

They walked down the hallway together, the girl moving more slowly than usual so Ben could keep up with her. He was still very sore, but his punctured lung was healing well. The headaches were still bad sometimes, especially after the dream, but he had come out of it reasonably well. Much better, in fact, than two of the people he'd met here at Lazarus House. One of those would need a cane the rest of his life.

"Good," he said. He repeated the word, pleased with the way it sounded. "Good."

They passed three more doorways leading to rooms much like his. "This place needs a cellular phone," he panted, stopping for a moment to rest.

The corners of her mouth flickered and he was pleased. It was the first time he had seen her smile.

"You're just pushing for a room near the lobby," she teased softly, then was gone.

He began moving again, his steps taking him to the top of the stairway that wound down to the first floor. Lazarus House had been a private home built by a retired sea captain in the early 1900s, and his love of natural wood was evident everywhere. Carefully descending the stairs, Ben once again got the feeling he was inside the hull of a ship, massive beams supporting the ceiling overhead while solid oak panels graced the walls. The captain's daughter, who had bequeathed the house to Kings County Family and Children's Services, had stipulated that, whatever changes were made, the natural wood should remain. Ben was glad the architects had honoured that request. It was a magnificent building, nothing like he expected.

Actually, he couldn't remember what he expected. When he was recuperating in the hospital, all he could think about was how ashamed he was. Everyone knew now. Ann's mother. The kids at school. His teachers. Everyone. He had refused visitors. For a while he had wanted to die.

But that was before he'd discovered who had placed the call that brought the police to North Street that last afternoon. It wasn't Mr. Lewis, although the teacher had been on the phone with the RCMP minutes after the initial call came in. Nor was it Ann whose feeling of foreboding had made her force her mother to turn off the 102 so she could get to a phone. The police had come immediately following the call his mother had made from Sadie's house.

His mother had gone to work that day wearing a bandana around her head. While it didn't completely hide the bruise on the side of her face, it cast a shadow that made it less obvious. She'd long since become, she realized, expert in the art of covering things up.

What she couldn't cover up, though, was how distracted she felt. She'd been upset before when Rankin used his hands against them, try as she might to make things smooth, make things even. But that afternoon she was distraught, frightened and angry with herself for having struck her son. As bad as things had ever been, she'd never laid a hand on him. She'd had no need to. He was a good boy. And she'd had no need to that day, either. He had only spoken aloud the things she knew in her own heart to be true.

And her heart had revealed yet another truth that day — that there was, perhaps, something even worse than being left alone after all. It was the look of betrayal she'd seen in her son's eyes.

At Save-Easy that afternoon, she'd entered prices incorrectly in the cash register, her trembling fingers faltering over the electronic keypad. She'd mixed up the tags on the pick-up bins so that Colin, the bag-boy, had loaded the wrong groceries into customers' vehicles. When Mr. Wile spoke to her about it she'd nearly wept, apologizing profusely. When he took her into his office and asked if anything was wrong, she did weep, softly, for a long time. Embarrassed, he had told her to go home, that they could manage without her the rest of the afternoon.

But she hadn't gone home. Seeing the LTD parked in the driveway she'd gone instead to Sadie's, arriving just as the old woman was preparing to leave for her women's group. She had sat in Sadie's kitchen holding an unopened diet Coke nearly half an hour before she trusted herself to speak, yet still it had come in great wracking sobs, a flood of words that could not be stopped. She'd told Sadie everything: the years of pain, of degradation, of shame. Her desperate efforts to be both a good mother and a good wife. Her struggle between her love for her son and her fear of losing everything all over again.

And the old woman had let her talk, had held her hand while the flood poured over her and around her, then had wrapped her sore arms around Ben's mother while she cried and cried and cried. Finally Sadie had spoken, her voice thick and low. "Child," she'd said, looking at the marks on the side of her friend's face, "men don't beat women because they love them. They beat them because they *can.*" She'd grimaced as if imagining the sounds the "off" switch on her hearing aid had made inaudible, then went on. "You can walk away from this. You're strong." Still sobbing, Ben's mother had shaken her head but Sadie had kept on. "There's a strength in you that you don't even know. Look what you've lived through already. You don't need that man. You can do anything you have to. Anything."

The sobs in the kitchen had quieted and they'd sat in silence for several more moments. Finally, Sadie had said, "The good Lord gave us minds so we could make choices. You make your choice, child."

And she'd made her choice, had dialled the Brookdale detachment of the RCMP while Sadie stood beside her, her gnarled brown hand squeezing her own.

She'd intended to wait for them there, to make sure this was finished before Ben arrived home. But then she'd looked out Sadie's porch door just as Ben was slipping inside their kitchen and everything had fallen apart. She'd dialled the police again with shaking hands, screaming into the phone for them to come, to please come, dear God, please come NOW, and then she had run like a deer from Sadie's house to her own.

And now, at last, it was over.

At the bottom of the stairs Ben looked left into what used to be a parlour but now served as a meeting room for the people whose home Lazarus House became for a time. Four women sat around a table drinking coffee. One of them was his mother and spread in front of her were several books and papers — bricks and mortar of the new life she and Ben were building for themselves. She had, much to Ben's delight and pride, decided to return to school, spending the past week preparing for her grade-equivalency test while waiting for summer courses to begin at the community college. And, with the help of one of the Lazarus counsellors, she had landed a part-time job with a printing company a few minutes' walk from the House. Soon they would even be able to think about a cheap apartment.

Although Kentville was a half-hour drive from Brookdale and Ann, Ben knew this town was their home, at least for a while. It was a chance to start over on their own terms, something he and his mother had been denied all their lives. Even Edgartown had been an end of a journey. Kentville was a beginning.

Besides, Ann had gotten her driver's licence while Ben was in the hospital, and it was she who had driven him to Lazarus House the day the doctor released him. And she'd been there half a dozen times since then, thanks to her mother who had been surprisingly generous with the Celica. In fact, he expected Ann to arrive any minute now, so he knew she wasn't the person waiting on the phone.

He walked across the hall to the two phones in the foyer and picked up the receiver that dangled in midair. "Hello?"

He listened to the hollow silence on the other end, expecting once again to hear the click and then the dial tone. There had been three other such calls in the week he'd been there, and he'd grown tired of the nuisance. It was a long way up and down those stairs.

"Hello?" he repeated again, but his hand was already reaching to break the connection.

"Hello." The voice was so faint Ben could not be sure if it was his caller or one of the shadow-voices you sometimes heard when conversations crossed on telephone wires.

"Hello. Who is this?"

There was another silence. Then, "How are you doing?" The voice was that of a male, someone Ben's age or slightly older.

Ben hesitated, trying to pull that voice from his memory. "Fine. I'm fine," he said.

"I heard what happened," the voice said. There was a pause and Ben resisted the impulse to fill the silence. Then, "It must have been terrible."

Ben said nothing for what seemed a very long time. Finally, "Yes. It was." The time for lies had long since passed.

"What got you through it?"

Ben remembered the dream he'd had the

night before last, the fourth time since he'd come to Lazarus House. "I'm not through it yet," he said quietly. "But I'm getting there."

The caller cleared his throat and Ben imagined him pulling words out of his belly, pushing each one separately into his own receiver. "I never got to say what I wanted to that day."

Something in the caller's tone and inflection seemed familiar, the words in Ben's head like seeds seeking newly turned earth. He listened to them echo soundlessly in his mind and he groped for a context that would give them meaning. When he had all but given up, a sudden tendril of memory thrust its way into his consciousness and Ben's eyes widened in astonishment. "Shay? Is that you?"

There was another pause, this one longer, and Ben was certain any moment he'd hear the click and the tone. But finally the words began again, slowly, as if each one was spoken at a price. "I wanted to apologize for what my father did. He had no right to say those things to you. He just —" Shay's voice trailed off, but Ben gave him the silence he needed. "He just loses his temper sometimes."

Ben suddenly saw again the yellow bloom on Shay's face that morning in front of the lockers. A dozen things raced through his mind, some of them he'd already written on paper, others he'd said aloud just to see how they sounded. All of them he'd imagined having been said to himself, words that might have ended the nightmare long before its conclusion. In the end, though, he said none of these. "What's getting *you* through it?" he asked gently.

There was a sound at the other end of the line. Ben waited. He waited a long time.

"Between his practice and his business deals, he's under a lot of stress." The sound came again. "I don't make it easier for him. I could do better. I'm trying to do better."

Ben spoke carefully. "It's not you, Shay. It's *never* been you. I know. My mother knows now, too." He swallowed thickly, remembering his mother softly singing "Amazing Grace" the other night while she helped prepare supper: . . . *was blind, but now I see.* "We learned it the hard way."

There was nothing for a while. Through an open window came the rumble of a car driving down the street, a low hum that built to a sudden wash of sound then droned on down into nothing. The sound reminded Ben of the snarl and whine of Freemont's huge saws, and he thought again of the logs that had been dropped and rolled and ripped and cut, yet emerged from the mill objects of value. "Shay," he said, "you've got to believe in yourself, believe that you matter. That you don't deserve what's happening to you. For a long time I didn't know that was true."

He thought of the first person who had told him that, Peter MacIssac, whose report about suspected abuse had come up on the RCMP's computer when the police booked Rankin that afternoon. Someday soon he intended to call

Pastor Pete. And Mr. Lewis, too.

"Shay," he continued, "you've got to have faith that there are people who understand." He hesitated, reaching for words, and through the curtain of his memory came something his mother had said but he only now understood. *Faith is the assurance of things hoped for, the conviction of things not seen.* "You're not alone, Shay, no matter what it feels like most of the time."

There was a straining sound on the other end, like someone lifting lead. "But how —" Silence. "What can —" He stopped. He seemed unable to go further.

"You need to tell," Ben said quietly. "There are people who can help."

Ben waited. Finally, "Shay? Are you still there?"

Suddenly the voice was different, that of another Shay. The Shay who didn't look back that first day Ben walked into Mr. Branigan's grade ten homeroom. The Shay who didn't say hello that early fall morning on the steps of the school. "Look, I have to go." Then, "Take care of yourself."

And then the click.

Ben looked at the receiver in his hand for a long time before placing it in its cradle, all the while imagining a tall, blond young man holding a similar receiver a world away, except his receiver would be a decorator colour, unusual and elegant. Ben imagined the perfect room in which that young man stood, then the perfect lawn under perfect trees just beyond that room. And he remembered the time a thousand years ago when he'd wished he were that young man.

He shook his head sadly, then hung up the phone and went out on the front step to wait for Ann.